ASTRAY

ALSO BY EMMA DONOGHUE

Room

Inseparable: Desire Between Women in Literature

The Sealed Letter

Landing

Touchy Subjects

Life Mask

The Woman Who Gave Birth to Rabbits

Slammerkin

Kissing the Witch: Old Tales in New Skins

Hood

Stir-fry

ASTRAY

EMMA DONOGHUE

PICADOR

First published 2012 by Little, Brown and Company,
a division of Hachette Book Group, Inc., New York

First published in Great Britain 2012 by Picador
an imprint of Pan Macmillan, a division of Macmillan Publishers Limited
Pan Macmillan, 20 New Wharf Road, London N1 9RR
Basingstoke and Oxford
Associated companies throughout the world
www.panmacmillan.com

ISBN 978-1-4472-0949-2

3 5 7 9 8 6 4 2

A CIP catalogue record for this book is available from
the British Library.

Printed and bound by CPI Group (UK) Ltd, Croydon, CR0 4YY

*For my seven far-flung siblings
(Dave, Helen, Hugh, Celia,
Mark, Barbara, Stella),
with love always.*

Tell us underneath what skies,
Upon what coasts of earth we have been cast;
We wander, ignorant of men and places,
And driven by the wind and the vast waves.

Virgil, The Aeneid,
translated by Allen Mandelbaum (1971)

CONTENTS

CONTENTS

DEPARTURES

LONDON

1882

MAN AND BOY

Off your tuck this morning, aren't you? That's not like you. It's the chill, perhaps. These March winds come straight from the Urals, up the Thames, or so they say. No, that's not your favorite Horse Guards playing, can't fool you; you never like it when they change the band. Fancy a bun? You'll feel the better for a good breakfast. Come along, have a couple of buns.... Please yourself, then.

Maybe later, after your bath.

I had some unpleasantness with the superintendent this morning. Yes, over you, my boy, need you ask? He's applied to the trustees for permission to buy a gun.

Calm down, no one's going to shoot you, or my name's not Matthew Scott. But let it be a warning. I don't mean to lay blame, but this is what comes of tantrums. (*Demented rampages,* the superintendent calls them.) Look at this old patched wall here; who was it that stove it in? To err is human and all that, but it don't excuse such an exhibition. You only went and hurt yourself, and you're still not the better for that abscess.

Anyway, the superintendent has an iddy-fix that you're a danger to the kiddies, now you're a man, as it were. Oh, you know and I know that's all my eye, you dote on the smalls. You don't care for confinement, that's all, and who can blame you? I can always settle you with a little wander round the Gardens to meet your friends. But the superintendent says, "What if you're off the premises, Scott, when the musth next comes on Jumbo? No other keeper here can handle him; every time I assign you an assistant, the creature terrorizes the fellow and sends him packing. It's a most irregular state of affairs, not to mention the pungency, and stains, and ... well, engorgement. That member's wife almost fainted when she caught sight!"

I pointed out you could hardly help that.

"Besides, bull Africans are known for killing their keepers," he lectured me. "In one of his furies, he could swat you down with his little tail, then crush you with his skull."

"Not this elephant," I said, "nor this keeper."

Then he went off on a gory story about a crazed elephant he saw gunned down in the Strand when he was knee-high, 152 bullets it took, the superintendent's never been the same since. Well, that explains a lot about him.

I assure you, my boy, I stood up for you. I looked the old man in the watery eye and said, "We all have our off days. But Jumbo's a cleanly, hardworking fellow, as a rule. I have never felt afraid of him for one moment in the seventeen years he's been in my care."

He muttered something impertinent about that proving my arrogance rather than your safety. "I believe it's gone to your head, Scott."

"What has, Superintendent?"

"Jumbo's fame. You fancy yourself the cock of the walk."

I drew myself up. "If I enjoy a certain position in this establishment, if I was awarded a medal back in 'sixty-six, that is due to having bred, nursed, and reared more exotic animals and birds than any other living man."

He pursed his lips. "Not to mention the fortune you pocket from those tuppenny rides—"

The nerve! "Aren't I the one who helps the kiddies up the ladder, and leads Jumbo round the Gardens, and makes sure they don't topple off?" (By rights the cash should be half yours, lad, but what use would it be to you? You like to mouth the coins with your trunk and slip them into my pocket.)

The superintendent plucked at his beard. "Be that as it may, it's inequitable; bad for morale. You're all charm when it earns you tips, Scott, but flagrantly rude to your superiors in this Society, and as for your fellow keepers, they're nervous of saying a word to you these days."

That crew of ignorami!

"I have plenty of conversation," I told him, "but I save it for those as appreciate it."

"They call you a tyrant."

Well, I laughed. After all, I'm the fifteenth child of seventeen, no silver spoons in my infant mouth, a humble son of toil who's made good in a precarious profession, and I need apologize to nobody. We don't mind the piddling tiddlers of this world, do we, boy? We just avert our gaze.

*   *   *

There's a crate sitting outside on the grass this morning. Pitch-pine planking, girded with iron, on a kind of trolley with wheels. Gives me a funny feeling. It's twelve feet high, as near as I can guess; that's just half a foot more than you. Nobody's said a word to me about it. Best to mind my own business, I suppose. This place—there's too much gossip and interference already.

It'll be time to stretch a leg soon, boy. The kiddies will be lined up outside in their dozens. They missed you yesterday, when it was raining. Here, kneel down and we'll get your howdah on. Yes, yes, I'll remember to put a double fold of blanket under the corner where it was rubbing. Aren't your toenails looking pearly after that scrub I gave them?

There's two men out there by the crate now, setting up some kind of ramp. I don't like the looks of this at all. If this is what I think it is, it's too blooming much—

I'm off to the superintendent's office, none of this *Please make an appointment.* Here's a sack of oats to be getting on with. Oh, don't take on, hush your bellowing, I'll be back before you miss me.

Well, Jumbo, I could bloody spit! Pardon my French, but there are moments in a man's life on this miserable earth—

And to think, the superintendent didn't give me so much as a word of warning. Just fancy, after all these years of working at the Society together—after the perils he and I have run, sawing off that rhinoceros's deformed horn and whatnot—it makes me shudder, the perfidiousness of it. "I'll thank you," says I, "to tell me what's afoot in the matter of my elephant."

"Yours, Scott?" says he with a curl of the lip.

"Figure of speech," says I. "As keeper here thirty-one years, man and boy, I take a natural interest in all property of the Society."

He was all stuff and bluster, I'd got him on the wrong foot. "Since you inquire," says he, "I must inform you that Jumbo is now the property of another party."

Didn't I stare! "Which other party?"

His beard began to tremble. "Mr. P. T. Barnum."

"The Yankee showman?"

He couldn't deny it. Then wasn't there a row, not half. My dear boy, I can hardly get the words out, but he's only been and gone and sold you to the circus!

It's a shocking smirch on the good name of the London Zoological Society, that's what I say. Such sneaking, double-dealing treachery behind closed doors. In the best interests of the British public, my hat! Two thousand pounds, that's the price the superintendent put on you, though it's not as if they need the funds, and who's the chief draw but the Children's Pal, the Beloved Pachydermic Behemoth, as the papers call you? Why, you may be the most magnificent elephant the world has ever seen, due to falling so fortuitously young into my hands as a crusty little stray, to be nursed back from the edge of the grave and fed up proper. And who's to say how long your poor tribe will last, with ivory so fashionable? The special friend of our dear queen as well as generations of young Britons born and unborn, and yet the Society has flogged you off like horse meat, and all because of a few whiffs and tantrums!

Oh, Jumbo. You might just settle down now. Your feelings do you credit and all that, but there's no good in such displays. You must be a brave boy. You've got through worse before, haven't you? When the traders gunned down your whole kin in front of you—

Hush now, my mouth, I shouldn't bring up painful recollections. Going into exile in America can't be half as bad, that's all I mean. Worse things happen. Come to think of it, if I hadn't rescued you from that wretched Jardin des Plantes, you'd have got eaten by hungry Frogs during the Siege of Seventy-one! So best to put a brave face on.

I just hope you don't get seasick. I reminded the superintendent you'd need two hundred pounds of hay a day on the voyage to New York, not to speak of sweet biscuits, potatoes, loaves, figs, and onions, your favorite.... You'll be joining the Greatest Show on Earth, I suppose that has a sort of ring to it, if a vulgar one. (The superintendent claims travel may calm your rages, or if it doesn't, then such a huge circus will have "facilities for seclusion," though I don't like the sound of that, not half.) No tricks to learn, I made sure of that much: you'll be announced as "The Most Enormous Land Animal in Captivity" and walk round the ring, that's all. I was worried you'd have to tramp across the whole United States, but you'll tour in your own comfy railway carriage, fancy that! The old millionaire's got twenty other elephants, but you'll be the king. Oh, and rats, I told him to pass on word that you're tormented by the sight of a rat ever since they ate half your feet when you were a nipper.

Of course you'll miss England, and giving the kiddies

rides, that's only to be expected. And doing headstands in the Pool, wandering down the Parrot Walk, the Carnivora Terrace, all the old sights. You'll find those American winters a trial to your spirits, I shouldn't wonder. And I expect once in a while you'll spare a thought for your old pa—

When you came to London, a filthy baby no taller than me, you used to wake screaming at night and sucking your trunk for comfort, and I'd give you a cuddle and you'd start to leak behind the ears…

Pardon me, boy, I'm overcome.

Today's the evil day, Jumbo, I believe you know it. You're all a-shiver, and your trunk hovers in front of my face as if to take me in. It's like some tree turned hairy snake, puffing warm wet air on me. There, there. Have a bit of gingerbread. Let me give your leg a good hard pat. Will I blow into your trunk, give your tongue a last little rub?

Come along, bad form to keep anyone waiting, I suppose, even a jumped-up Yankee animal handler like this "Elephant Bill" Newman. (Oh, those little watery eyes of yours, lashes like a ballet dancer—I can hardly look you in the face.) That's a boy; down this passage to the left; I know it's not the usual way, but a change is as good as a rest, don't they say? This way, now. Up the little ramp and into the crate you go. Plenty of room in there, if you put your head down. Go on.

Ah, now, let's have no nonsense. Into your crate this minute. What good will it do to plunge and bellow? No, stop it, don't lie down. Up, boy, up. Bad boy. Jumbo!

*   *   *

You're all right, don't take on so. You're back in your quarters for the moment; it's getting dark out. Such a to-do! They're only chains. I know you dislike the weight of them, but they're temporary. No, I can't take them off tonight or this Elephant Bill will raise a stink. He says we must try you again first thing tomorrow. The chains are for securing you inside the crate, till the crane hoists you on board the steamer. No, calm down, boy. Enough of that roaring. Drink your scotch. Oi! Pick up my bowler and give it back. Thank you.

The Yankee, Elephant Bill, has some cheek. He began by informing me that Barnum's agents tried to secure the captured King of the Zulus for exhibition, and then the cottage where Shakespeare was born; you're only their third choice of British treasures. Well, I bristled, you can imagine.

When you wouldn't walk into the crate no matter how we urged and pushed, even after he took the whip to your poor saggy posterior—when I'd led you round the corner and tried again half a dozen times—he rolled his eyes, said it was clear as day you'd been spoiled.

"Spoiled?" I repeated.

"Made half pet, half human," says the American, "by all these treats and pattings and chit-chat. Is it true what the other fellows say, Scott, that you share a bottle of whiskey with the beast every night, and caterwaul like sweethearts, curled up together in his stall?"

Well, I didn't want to dignify that kind of impertinence

with a reply. But then I thought of how you whine like a naughty child if I don't come back from the pub by bedtime, and a dreadful thought occurred to me. "Elephants are family-minded creatures, you must know that much," I told him. "I hope you don't mean to leave Jumbo alone at night? He only sleeps two or three hours, on and off; he'll need company when he wakes."

A snort from the Yank. "I don't bed down with nobody but human females."

Which shows the coarseness of the man.

Settle down, Jumbo, it's only three in the morning. No, I can't sleep neither. I haven't had a decent kip since that blooming crate arrived. Don't those new violet-bottomed mandrills make an awful racket?

Over seven thousand visitors counted at the turnstile today. All because of you, Jumbo. Your sale's been in the papers; you'd hardly credit what a fuss it's making. Heartbroken letters from kiddies, denunciations of the trustees, offers to raise a subscription to ransom you back. It's said the Prince of Wales has voiced his objections, and Mr. Ruskin, and some Fellows of the Society are going to court to prove the sale illegal!

I wish you could read some of the letters you're getting every day now, from grown-ups as well as kiddies. Money enclosed, and gingerbread, not to mention cigars. (I ate the couple of dozen oysters, as I knew you wouldn't fancy them.) A bun stuck with pins; that's some sot's idea of a joke. And look at this huge floral wreath for you to wear, with a banner that says A TROPHY OF TRIUMPH OVER THE AMERICAN SLAVERS. I've had letters myself, some offering me bribes to "do something to prevent this," others calling me a Judas. If they only knew the mortifications of my position!

Oh, dear, I did think today's attempt would have gone better. It was my own idea that since you'd taken against the very sight of the crate, it should be removed from view. I told this Elephant Bill I'd lead you through the streets, the full six miles, and surely by the time you reached the docks, you'd be glad to go into your crate for a rest.

But you saw right through me, didn't you, artful dodger? No, no tongue massage for you tonight, Badness! You somehow knew this wasn't an ordinary stroll. Not an inch beyond the gates of the Gardens but you dropped to your knees. Playing to the crowd, rather, I thought, and how they whooped at the sight of you on all fours like some plucky martyr for the British cause. The public's gone berserk over your *sit-down strike,* you wouldn't believe the papers.

I almost lost my temper with you today at the gates, boy, when you wouldn't get up for me, and yet I couldn't help but feel a sort of pride to see you put up such a good fight.

That Yank is a nasty piece of work. When I pointed out that it might prove impossible to force you onto that ship, he muttered about putting you on low rations to damp your spirit, or even bull hooks to the ears and hot irons.

"I'll have you know, we don't stand for that kind of barbarism in this country," I told him, and he grinned and said the English were more squeamish about beating their animals than their children. He showed me a gun he carries and drawled something about getting you to New York dead or alive.

The lout was just trying to put the wind up me, of course. Primitive tactics. "Jumbo won't be of much use to your employer if he's in the former state," says I coldly.

Elephant Bill shrugged, and said he didn't know about that, Barnum could always stuff your hide and tour it as "The Conquered Briton."

That left me speechless.

Will we take a stroll round the Gardens this morning before the gates open? Over eighteen thousand visitors yesterday, and as many expected today, to catch what might be a last glimpse of you. Such queues for the rides! We could charge a guinea apiece if we chose, not that we would.

Let's you and me go and take a look at your crate. It's nothing to be afraid of, idiot boy; only a big box. Look, some fresh writing since yesterday: *Jumbo don't go,* that's kind. More flowers. Dollies, books, even. See that woman on her knees outside the gates? A lunatic, but the civil kind. She's handing out leaflets and praying for divine intervention to stop your departure.

But the thing is, lad, you're going to have to go sooner or later. You know that, don't you? There comes a time in every man's life when he must knuckle down and do the necessary. The judge has ruled your sale was legal. Barnum's told the *Daily Telegraph* he won't reconsider, not for a hundred thousand pounds. So the cruel fact is that our days together are numbered. Why not step on into your crate now, this very minute, get the wrench of parting over, since it must come to that in the end? Quick, now, as a favor to your sorrowful pa? Argh! Be that way, then; suit yourself, but don't blame me if the Yank comes at you with hooks and irons.

It's like trying to move a mountain, sometimes. Am I your master or your servant, that's what I want to know? It's a queer business.

That superintendent! To think I used to be amused by his little ways, almost fond of the old gent. Well, a colder fish I never met. Sits there in his dusty top hat and frock coat flecked with hippopotami's whatsits, tells me he's giving me a little holiday.

"A holiday?" I was taken aback, as you can imagine. I haven't taken a day off in years, you'd never stand for it.

He fixes me with his yellowing eyes and tells me that my temporary removal will allow Mr. Newman to accustom himself to the elephant's habits and tastes before departure.

"You know Jumbo's tastes already," I protest. "He can't stand that Yank. And if the fellow dares to try cruel measures, word will get out and you'll have the police down on you like a shot, spark off riots, I shouldn't wonder."

Which sends the superintendent off on a rant about how I've been conspicuously unwilling to get you into that crate.

"Oh, I like that," says I. "I've only loaded the unfortunate creature with shackles, pushed and roared to drive all six and a half tons of him into that blooming trap, so how is it my fault if he won't go?"

He fixes me with a stare. "Mr. Newman informs me that you must be engaging in sabotage, by giving the elephant secret signals. I have suspected as much on previous occasions, when I sent you perfectly competent assistants and Jumbo ran amok and knocked them down like ninepins."

"Secret signals?" I repeat, flabbergasted.

"All I know is that your hold over that beast is uncanny," says the superintendent between his teeth.

Uncanny? What's uncanny about it? Nothing more natural than that you'd have a certain regard for your pa, after he's seen to all your little wants day and night for the last seventeen years. Why does the lamb love Mary so, and all that rot.

Well, boy, at that moment I hear a little click in my head. It's like at the halls when a scene flies up and another one descends. I suddenly say—prepare yourself, lad—I say, "Then why don't you send a telegraph to this Barnum and tell him to take me too?"

The superintendent blinks.

"I'm offering my services as Jumbo's keeper," says I, "as long as his terms are liberal."

"What makes you imagine Mr. Barnum would hire such a stubborn devil as you, Scott?"

That threw me, but only for a second. "Because he must be a stubborn devil himself to have paid two thousand pounds for an elephant he can't get onto the ship."

A long stare, and the superintendent says, "I knew I was right. You have been thwarting me all along, using covert devices to keep Jumbo in the zoo."

I smirked, letting him believe it. Covert devices, my eye! To the impure, all things are impure. "Just you send that tele- graph," I told him, "and you'll be soon rid of both of us."

Now, now, boy, let me explain. Doesn't it strike you that we've had enough of England? Whoa! No chucking your filth on the walls, that's a low habit. Hear me out. I know what a patriotic heart you've got—specially considering you come from the French Sudan, not our Empire at all—but how have you been repaid? Yes, the plain people dote on you, but it strikes me that you've grown out of these cramped quarters. If the Society's condemned you to transportation for smashing a few walls and shocking a few members' wives, why, then—let's up stakes and be off to pastures new, I say. You're not twenty-one yet, and I'm not fifty. We're self-made prodigies, come up from nothing and now headline news. We can make a fresh start in the land of the free and home of the brave. We'll be ten times as famous, and won't England feel the loss of us, won't Victoria weep!

I expect the superintendent will call me in right after lunch, the wonders of modern telegraphy being what they are. (Whatever Barnum offers me, I'll accept it. The Society can kiss my you-know-exactly-what-I-mean.) I'll come straight back here and lead you out to the crate. Now, whatever you do, Jumbo, don't make a liar of me. I don't have any secret signals or hidden powers; all I can think to do is to walk into the crate first, and turn, and open my arms and call you. Trust me, dearest boy, and I'll see you safe across the ocean, and stay by your side for better for worse, and take a father's and mother's care of you till the end. Are you with me?

Man and Boy

This story is based on almost daily reports in the *Times* of London between January and April 1882, as well as Superintendent Abraham Bartlett's hostile account in his *Wild Animals in Captivity* (1898), and the ghostwritten 1885 *Autobiography of Matthew Scott, Jumbo's Keeper*. Even after Matthew Scott persuaded Jumbo into his crate, the controversy—nicknamed "Jumbomania" or "the Jumbo movement"—lingered for several months on both sides of the Atlantic, inspiring songs, poems, jokes, cartoons, advertisements, and the sale of "Jumbo" cigars, collars, fans, earrings, perfume, and ice cream.

Jumbo toured with Barnum's troupe over four very successful seasons (and showed no further sign of the aggression that dental analysis now suggests can be blamed on impacted molars, due to his low-fiber diet). In 1885, as Scott led him across a railway track after a performance in St. Thomas, Ontario, the elephant was killed by an unscheduled freight train. Barnum rehired Scott for one more season to introduce audiences to Jumbo's stuffed hide. Despite pressure to return to England, Scott hung on near the circus's winter headquarters in Bridgeport, Connecticut, where he died in 1914 in the almshouse, aged around eighty. Jumbo's hide was lost in a fire, but his skeleton lies in storage at the American Museum of Natural History, in New York.

LONDON
1854

ONWARD

Caroline always prepares Fred's breakfast herself. Her young brother's looking sallow around the eyes. "We saved you the last of the kippers," she says in a tone airy enough to give the impression that she and Pet had their fill of kippers before he came down this morning.

Mouth full, Fred sings to his niece in his surprising bass.

> *His brow is wet with honest sweat,*
> *He earns whate'er he can*
> *And looks the whole world in the face*
> *For he owes not any man.*

Pet giggles at the face he's pulling. Caroline slides her last triangle of toast the child's way. Pet's worn that striped frock since spring. Is she undersized for two years old? But then girls are generally smaller. Are the children Caroline sees thronging the parks equally twiglike under their elaborate coats? "Where did you pick that one up?" she asks Fred.

"A fellow at the office."

"Again, again," insists Pet: her new word this week.

Caroline catches herself watching the clock.

Fred launches into song again as he rises to his feet and brushes the crumbs from his waistcoat with a manner oddly middle-aged for twenty-three.

> *Toiling,—rejoicing,—sorrowing,*
> *Onward through life he goes...*

"Come, now, Pet, let Uncle get his coat on." Fred mustn't be late, but that's not it: Caroline wants him gone so she can tackle the day. The child, windmill-armed, slaps imaginary dust out of her uncle's trousers while her mother adjusts his collar. Not that there's any real prospect of advancement from the ranks of draftsmen, but still, no harm in looking dapper. She nearly made an architect of him, so very nearly; another few years would have done it. *Nearly never knit a sock,* as their mother used to say in sober moments.

"Bye-bye," chants Pet, "bye-bye, bye-bye."

Fred always leaves to catch his omnibus with a cheerful expression. Does he like his work? she wonders. Or does he just put a brave face on it for twenty-five shillings a week?

Caroline carries the tray down to the kitchen and leaves the dishes for the girl. Pet drops a saucer, but by some miracle it only spins loudly on the tiles. Upstairs to do the beds together, shaking out the blankets; Caroline straightens everything as soon as her daughter's back is turned. Then down to the parlor again, where she takes up her mending while Pet wreaks havoc in the sewing box. The room is cooling down as the fire goes gray.

Fred needs new cuffs. These ones are so frayed, it would

be throwing good thread after bad to darn them. Or that's her excuse; Caroline's fingers are stupid with the needle. Her little brother, her charge and her pride, and she sends him out every day a little shabbier. Toast crumbs still gritty in her throat, and already Caroline is reviewing the contents of the pantry, brooding over lunch. The remains of yesterday's beef? "What a tall tower," she marvels, watching Pet set another spool on top of the quivering structure. Spools crash and roll across the room. Caroline jumps, pricks herself. "Pick up now" is all she lets herself say, sucking her finger. "Good girl," she cries when her daughter produces the last dust-rimmed spool from under the table. Is false cheer better than none? she wonders. So much of motherhood is acting.

Usually she manages to get Pet down to sleep by noon, when the girl comes in to mind her, but today Pet's wound up, squeaking in her own private language, rattling buttons in the tin.

A confident knock at the door. Early, how can he be this early, before the maid's even got here? What makes him believe, what gives him the right—

Anger tightens the drawstrings of Caroline's face. "A visitor for Mamma! Would you like to sit here quiet as a mouse and play with Mamma's jewels?" Before she's finished speaking, she's thundering up to her room, taking the stairs two at a time, Pet stumbling in her wake.

She grabs the jewelry box from her dressing table. The second knock, still sprightly. He'll wait, won't he? Surely he'll give her a minute to get to the blasted door—

As she reaches the hall again, passing the struggling child

on the stairs, her skirt almost knocks Pet over; Caroline grabs the small hand and pulls her into the parlor. She's breathing hard as she sets the jewelry box down on the sofa. Pet's mouth forms an O of ecstasy. All that's left are cheap necklaces and bracelets in glass and jet, probably easy enough to break, but then again, not valuable enough to matter. "Be good now, Pet." *Good,* what does that mean to a two-year-old whose every natural urge is to poke, to grab, to take the world in her fists and shake the secrets out of it? The fire— Caroline slams the guard across it. "Mamma back soon!"

The third knock hammers as she's dashing through the hall; she pauses to shake her skirts into shape.

Her smiling apologies overlap with his. This one's all bluff humor and compliments; he's brought what he calls a mere token. Caroline stares at the miniature lilies, hides her face in their white stiffness. The scent is sweet enough to hurt her throat. Eerie white bugles, suited to a girl's coffin. This late in the autumn, they must be hothouse blooms: she reckons the cost.

"Mamma!" Pet, lurching into the hall, heavy with necklaces.

"Stay in the parlor," says Caroline, picking her up, crushing her against the flowers. She plants her on the sofa again, and in the small perfect ear, very low and fierce, she says, "Sh!" Turns to find the visitor leaning in the doorway, grinning as if to demonstrate that he doesn't mind encountering the little one, on the contrary, in fact. It occurs to her that he's scanning Pet's features, and her stomach turns.

"Piddy," remarks Pet, caressing one glacial petal.

What's a pity? How does the child know about pity? Oh, *pretty*. Caroline yanks the bouquet away. "Yes, Mamma's special pretty flowers, don't touch."

Upstairs, she chats a little, marvels at how long her visitor's mustache is getting. Has he had a very tiresome morning in the City? He's considering investing in the Canadian Grand Trunk Railway, well, hasn't that quite a ring to it.

The sheets have a damp feel against her back, though Caroline tells herself she must be imagining it. She moves the way he prefers, with her ears always pricked. Nothing, not a sound. Could Pet have crept upstairs, might she be outside Mamma's bedroom door right now, plucking up her nerve to push the door open? No, no, Caroline would have heard something; one of those little gasps of exertion or nonsense words a two-year-old can't help making. But the man has put his oily mustache to her ear now, he's grunting like a seal. She can't hear anything else. She should be making those delicate bird cries he likes, but, oh god, what if a necklace has snagged, tightened round Pet's soft throat? Earrings, she forgot to take the damn earrings out of the box. What would one of those tiny sharp hooks do to a small stomach? Her fingers clamp on the pale meat of his shoulders. *Hurry, hurry, do your business and be done with it.*

"Oh, sweet Caroline," he groans.

A rage spirals up when she hears him use her name, a coal-smoke whirlwind wrenching this scarecrow out of her, hurling him against the walls, whipping him through the pealing glass to fall like rag 'n' bones on the Brompton street, where the next passing carriage will flatten his face into stone and mud.

A small sound brings her back to herself. Rocking away on top of her, the visitor doesn't notice, but Caroline can make out voices in the parlor, one deeper than the other. The girl at last, ten minutes late by the clock on the dresser. It's all right. Pet's all right. Caroline's teeth unlock.

Love fizzes like acid in her bones. She doesn't have to fake that.

Lunch is the last of the beef, in a soup, bulked out with turnips. Pet pushes her bowl away, but Caroline puts the spoon between the little pink lips over and over.

Though the child hasn't had her nap, Caroline takes her out while the rain is holding off. "Pam pam," wails Pet. Her memory is getting longer; the pram was pawned three weeks ago. (Uncle Fred doesn't seem to have noticed.)

"You're a great big girl now, you can walk," says Caroline with one of those smiles that are too hard around the edges. Pet wanders in long spirals, trips over a pine cone. "Come along, my sweet. This way." The air's bad today; damp and sulfurous. "On we go!" After a minute, Caroline dips to lift her daughter onto her hip. When they reach Brompton Park, Pet struggles to get down and chases sparrows with the lumbering merriment of a drunk. She coughs with excitement, picks up a branch covered in curled yellow leaves and shakes it like a standard. Caroline wonders if the brown boots are pinching. She thinks of Chinese ladies with their ghastly little feet. For winter she could always line that thin coat with a flannel petticoat of her own...but then it mightn't button up at the front.

"Birdies! Mamma, birdies!"

"That's right, pretty birdies."

A spattering of rain. On the way home, they pass two women on a bench, whose conversation halts. Eyes flicker then avert. The chat starts up again in graver tones.

Does Caroline hear her name? She keeps her gaze at the level of her daughter's face. "Look, a snail," she remarks inanely.

"Nail," echoes Pet, bending to examine it.

But her mother jerks her hand. "On we go, the rain's coming."

Caroline doesn't care what people say, not for herself. There's an automatic searing of the cheeks at moments like these; occasionally on waking, a leaden sense of her fate that presses her against the pillow. But no shame. What time in her day has she for shame?

"Nail," cries Pet again, squatting to reach for something that looks very like dog dirt.

"Time for cocoa," says Caroline, hauling her onto her hip with one arm.

Fallen. It's not like in the novels, or on the stage; it's as ordinary as darning. What has Caroline ever done but what she had to since she was nineteen and she found herself alone with a nine-year-old brother to raise? The road never seemed to fork. She's put one foot in front of another, and this is where they have led her, this moment, fat drops of rain falling into her collar, as she rushes along the blotched footpath with Pet laughing on her hip. Onward, onward, because backward is impossible. *Fallen,* like leaves that can't be stuck back on the trees again.

And it strikes Caroline now that everything the child learns is a step closer to misery. When will Pet begin to register the neighbors' words? At four? Five? Coming home with her face streaked with knowledge: *I heard a bad word.* Cruel misnamings of what she is, or rather, what her mother is; the falsity of fact. And what will Caroline tell her then? What fiction, what feeble justification? She wishes absurdly that Pet would stay light enough to carry on her hip; would shrink, in fact, falling back month by month into the plump oblivion of infancy.

At home, the afternoon goes smoothly: a small mercy. The girl takes Pet up for a nap, while Caroline glances at yesterday's paper. *STOWAWAY FOUND ACCIDENTALLY STIFLED IN SALT BARREL THREE DAYS OUT FROM LIVERPOOL,* says a headline; Caroline winces, and turns the page. She screws up her eyes to read tiny advertisements for items she can't afford.

By the time her second visitor knocks, Pet and the maid are playing with paper dolls in the parlor. This one only ever speaks about the weather; she agrees with him that the rain will get heavier before dark. Never more than three visitors a day, and usually only two; she can't cut down any more than that and still make the books balance. No strangers, no boors; she has her standards.

Caroline has bathed, and dismissed the girl, and tidied up, hours before Fred comes home soaked to the ankles. (She can't find the bouquet of lilies, though it lingers on the air; the girl must have thrown it out, a piece of quiet tact that surprises Caroline.) Her brother apologizes for being late; the rain always causes traffic jams. He likes the way she's moved the easy chair a little closer to the window. "It's these little touches," Fred assures her. "Lets me enjoy the view, while I'm polishing my shoes."

The view, as if their window looked onto an alpine lake, instead of one of Brompton's meaner terraces.

Pet's got him singing that song about the blacksmith again.

> *Toiling,—rejoicing,—sorrowing,*
> *Onward through life he goes . . .*

His voice is a little hoarser after the long day. It was her little brother, Fred, who taught her to be a mother, long before Pet. Love happens, like age or weather. It's not hard to do, only to endure, sometimes.

Caroline always asks about his work, though there's not much to say about the drawings on which he's engaged; mostly he passes on gossip about the architects. In return Fred inquires about her reading; he's created a sort of fiction that his sister's day is divided between the care of her child and intellectual advancement. (Caroline sometimes leaves a book on her desk for a few days, then returns it to the library unread. It is not that the visitors take up so much of her day, but until they are dealt with and banished to the other side of the front door again, she can't settle to anything else.)

She tries not to recall the moment four years ago when she told Fred his articles would have to be canceled; his face like a starched sheet. There's no one in particular to blame, which makes it worse. Not the man she lived with for nine years, seeing to his accounts as well as every other wifely duty; he would have gone on supporting her and her brother for the rest of his life, she's sure, had his business not failed. He'd have married her, in fact, if he hadn't had the bad luck to be married already. Caroline can't blame herself, either. When she was nineteen she gambled all she had, but hardly recklessly; for nine years it seemed a decent bargain. What did abstractions like honor matter compared with realities: white bread in a child's wet mouth?

"Tired, sis?"

"Not really," she says, rousing herself to smile. Fred still looks like a boy, especially when he puts on that avuncular face.

"Shall we have a game of cards?"

"Oh, yes," she says, mustering a tone of delight. Ersatz, every word, and yet all meant in good earnest.

"This is very snug," says Fred, poking the fire. "Nothing so jolly as an autumn evening in the bosom of the family."

She wishes he wouldn't overdo it. Every evening is just like this, unless there's some drama such as Pet coming down with mumps or a bird banging about in the chimney. They can't afford any amusements, and they have no friends. Fred claims to get on well enough with the other draftsmen, but he's never going to risk inviting one home to meet his "widowed" sister. As for Caroline, no woman of her own sort would know her, and she doesn't want to know the other sort. She lives in the crack between two worlds.

This cozy-nest stuff is not exactly a lie, though. More like a show: a play to entertain Pet. She's the one who knows least, and so matters most. Again, Caroline feels that queer impulse to shut those bright eyes with her hand, cover those shell-pink ears, close that curious mouth. To beckon her daughter back inside her. To squeeze her like a pearl locked up in its oyster. To—

No, not that. Caroline can never wish Pet unbegun. That's the paradox that tires her brain, strains her heart: the best thing in her life has sprung from the worst. So though Caroline can't bear her life, she wouldn't swap it for any other.

A heavy sweetness; she turns her head sharply.

"Piddy flower," Pet is saying, as she lays the bruised lilies across Fred's knee.

"Wherever did you get those pretty flowers?" marvels Fred.

"Mamma visitor," says Pet confidingly.

Caroline snatches the bouquet. Halfway down the stairs, she hears the house ring with Pet's shrieks. In the kitchen, the reek of the scrap bucket makes her retch, but it's better than the lilies. She pushes them down deep under the gristle and turnip peel, and scrubs her hands on the cloth.

"Sis—" Fred is holding Pet with her face pressed against his shirtfront; she's still gulping.

"Mamma's sorry," she tells Pet hoarsely, "but the flowers were dirty. They had to go in the bucket."

She tries to take the child, but Pet clings to her uncle with a fresh burst of wailing.

"I'll bring you some more tomorrow," Fred promises the child. "What about roses? Roses are ever so pretty."

"And ever so expensive," says Caroline under her breath, examining her nails.

"It's my money."

They stare at each other in the dim kitchen. After a second she reaches for Pet—unresisting now—and carries her upstairs.

Caroline takes longer than usual to go through the routine; she sings Pet half a dozen nursery rhymes and stays for a while after the lamp is turned down. They say it spoils a child to let them have a light at night, but Caroline doesn't care. If you break the cardinal rule when you're still a girl, what does it matter if you break a few more? *When the bough breaks, the cradle will fall,* she sings under her breath. *Down will come baby, cradle and all.*

Bone-weary: she's tempted to go to bed. But she can't leave Fred alone downstairs. Entering the parlor, she sits straight down and picks up her hand of cards.

Her brother's hand closes over hers. "Caro."

The old name saps her, melts her.

"What I said—"

"Of course your wages are your own," she tells him.

"Of course they're not. All for one, and all that. Besides, you earn twice what I do."

The word hits her hard. They've always spoken as if the figures Caroline adds to the household budget every week come from dividends, or a legacy. *Earn:* as if it were a job like any other. She feels mortification, and a strange sort of relief.

"Last week I applied for the position of ticket-collector at the Olympic," he goes on.

"Fred, you can't work in the evenings, too!"

He shrugs like a small boy. "Today I heard the position has been filled; there were more than thirty applicants."

She doesn't know what to say: *what a shame,* or *just as well.*

"We can't go on like this," he says, pursing his lips.

She stares at him.

"A new beginning, that's what we need, where nobody knows us. New surnames, even."

Caroline's eyes hurt as they rest on her brother. So young still, so wonderfully stupid. Not that her borrowed surname means anything to her; she'd change it in the morning if it would do any good. "Fred," she says softly, "that wouldn't work for long. In another part of London, or another town, even, the neighbors—they'd start to notice as soon as there were—" Her throat locks on the word *visitors.* "People coming and going," she finishes weakly.

Fred's jaw is set. "If I could get a better position, you could drop all that."

All that: only now, in the tightness of his words, can she hear how much he hates the men who have been swanning into his house since he was a child. She bites her lip. But what *better position?* Thirty men ahead of him for a job collecting theater tickets!

"I wouldn't mind getting into some other line altogether," he mentions. "Some business you could help me with, even; you've got a great head for figures."

She breathes out her exasperation before she speaks. "In such times as these, Fred—"

"I don't mean in England," he says, very low.

"Not in England?" She repeats it without understanding.

And then, unexpectedly, he grins. "If we made up our minds to a really fresh start...well, it could be anywhere. The Cape. Australia. Canada."

Caroline blinks. "You're proposing that—"

"Don't ask me for any details yet," he says, "but there are opportunities. Everyone says so. More space," he adds urgently, "and fewer people. Less fuss about one's origins, too."

She nods at that.

"Things are just getting started in those sorts of places," says Fred with a kind of wonder, "whereas here..."

"Things have been going on as they are for such a long time."

"Yes." He grips his sister's fingers hard enough to hurt. "Where should we go?"

"I—" She stops herself before she can say she doesn't care, or that it makes no difference, because it's not going to happen; it's a child's fantasy. "You choose."

"Could you bear it, really, Caro? Leaving England behind?"

What's the harm in humoring him?

"I expect I would hate it at first," she says quietly.

Fred's face falls.

"But I could get used to it, I believe. We all could, especially Pet." Her throat locks on the syllable. To really live. Not walled up.

"Oh, sis. A fresh start!"

"People do it every day," she says, a little giddy. Is she deluding herself that she could be anything but what she is? When you change countries, perhaps your old self stays fixed to your back, like a turtle's shell.

Fred is standing by the little writing desk. He lets out his breath in a half whistle and sits down on the beveled edge.

You'll break it, she wants to say, but she stops herself. Instead she says what just a moment ago she wasn't going to. "But it can't be done, Fred, not really."

His jaw juts, exactly like his niece's. "Why can't it?"

"Come, now. However would we raise the cost of our passage?"

"Ah, I have one or two ideas about that," he announces.

Caroline's eyes narrow. "Nothing reckless, Fred?"

"No, no. There's someone to whom I mean to write, to ask—"

"For charity?" she interrupts shrilly.

Her brother's fiddling with the pen she uses to keep the household books, rubbing dried ink off the nib. "This person's a very distinguished gentleman—I won't name him, in case nothing comes of it, but I know he takes an interest in such cases."

Such cases. That means her. A long pause, and Caroline considers the curiously lingering nature of pride. "You wouldn't tell this person? Tell him my story?" she forces herself to add.

"Ours. Our story. I would be obliged to tell it," he says, almost stern, coming over to the sofa and letting himself down beside her.

She squeezes her eyes shut.

"You have nothing to be ashamed of," Fred says.

Hot water spills down her face. What does he know?

"I'd put it all down on paper just once. To be done with it. Say I may?"

Sell her story, instead of her body? "No." Caroline's pulse is in her ears, as fast as the wheels of a train, as loud as a ship's engine. Not on and on, but out and away. To let out the truth, and then sink it under the waves. What will she tell Pet, years later? Nothing, nothing at all. Or a beautiful lie: *We lost your papa back in England.* "No," she says, "I'll do it," opening her eyes blindly and taking the pen from his hand.

Onward

Caroline Thompson's existence is recorded only in the letters of Charles Dickens. The young draftsman Frederick Maynard first wrote to the novelist about his older sister on October 10, 1854, and Dickens got to know both siblings before persuading his fellow philanthropist Angela Burdett-Coutts to set Caroline up with a lodging house. When that failed to make Caroline a living, he and Burdett-Coutts let her sell the furniture (for something more than a hundred pounds) to pay her and her child's way to Canada. Since on May 14, 1856, Dickens referred to "an endeavor I am making to do something to help a sister and brother to go out to Canada with some sort of light upon their way," it looks as if Fred went with his sister and niece. On September 26, 1857, Dickens recorded, "I saw Mrs. Thompson before she went, and told her that I trusted her with great confidence."

Fred's song is Henry Wadsworth Longfellow's "The Village Blacksmith" (1842).

NEW YORK CITY
1735

THE WIDOW'S CRUSE

It was peculiarly warm for an April morning. Huddlestone left his apartment and crossed Dock Street to the best coffeehouse in town. The young attorney nodded to a couple of wholesalers, but he took his coffee alone by the window, with the *New York Weekly Journal.*

There was a paragraph about some females down in Chester County who'd formed a sort of secret court to arraign a man who'd battered his wife over some trifle. They'd sentenced the fellow to be ducked three times in a pond, and shaved off half his hair and half his beard to make a laughingstock of him. Huddlestone grinned over this story but was not convinced; newsmen today would invent any nonsense to fill an inch of paper.

Two ships from Curaçao had just docked on the East River, he read. Missionary work among the Mohawk might prove a waste of Christian energies. One Scriblerus Despondus wrote to complain that no play had been mounted in two years, *the whole thoughts of the boorish freemen of New York being turned upon price and profit.* Huddlestone couldn't see that this constituted a problem. God knew, he hadn't followed his father into the law for love of Justice. He was an eager servant of Mammon, even if he hadn't yet been rewarded for it, since business was so damnably tight.

Huddlestone stared out the grimy window at the human traffic, spotting Highlander blow-ins and stern old Dutch, penniless Palatines and English infantrymen. Just about every second face was black. Huddlestone kept only a couple of indentured Irish himself, and he'd lost one of those in the smallpox epidemic. According to the *Weekly Journal,* the dreaded scarlatina was currently cutting a swath through the colonies of New England. Any reader who found red, itching pustules on his neck, face, or tongue was urged to be patriotic enough to board up self and family at once.

Having some bills to send out, the attorney drained his coffee to the grit, then crossed the road to his cramped office, yawning.

An hour later came an unexpected knock. Huddlestone jumped up and clapped his wig back on.

The sight of the widow's weeds made him deepen his bow. Her hoops were so wide that she had to execute a sideways maneuver to get through the door; the skirt was excellent black satin, pulled up through pocket-slits to keep it out of the mud. Linen mittens hid her hands, except for the narrow fingertips. Under the hood of her cape, the widow's face was sharply boned; not an Englishwoman, and no more than twenty-five, Huddlestone reckoned. At the edge of her crisp white cap, the darkness of her hair showed through the blue-gray flour.

She began to apologize for imposing on a perfect stranger.

"No imposition, madam, I assure you. A certain clique of

men keep such a grip on legal business in this city, the rest of us are always eager for new clients," he admitted disarmingly. "If it's as a client that you've come?"

She turned sharply toward the wall, as if to examine his diploma from Yale College.

Damn it, had Huddlestone somehow offended his visitor already? He pressed her to a glass of Madeira, but she shook her head, her face still averted. "Then, if I may ask, how may I be of assistance?"

When she turned back to him her powdered face was striped with tears.

"Madam—"

"My name is Mrs. Gomez," she said. "My husband was a merchant." Her throat moved as if she'd swallowed a stone.

Huddlestone should have guessed it, there was a certain tint under her pallor. Of course he'd heard of the Gomez clan: Sephardics from the West Indies, and among the more substantial fortunes in the little Mill Street congregation who'd recently erected the first purpose-built synagogue in the New World.

She spoke with difficulty. "He set off to Boston some weeks ago, to meet his trading partners."

"By sea?"

"By land."

Huddlestone winced. Country roads—if you could call them that—were only a foot or two wide, and bedeviled with Indians.

"A martyr to seasickness," she whispered.

"Ah."

"He—word reached me this week, that he got no farther than Connecticut," she gasped. After a moment, she brought out the words. "The scarlatina."

A nasty death. Huddlestone deepened his voice. "May I offer my deepest sympathies?"

Mrs. Gomez pressed her lace apron to her face for a moment. "I happened upon your sign," she said, her eyes lifting to his. "I was walking along. You must understand, I am quite friendless."

"Your kinsmen, surely..."

"They reside in Jamaica."

And her husband's, what of the Gomez family? But of course Huddlestone corrected himself, matters of inheritance were always delicate. "May I ask, have you children?"

She squeezed her eyes shut. "We were not so blessed."

Sharpening his quill, Huddlestone began to take notes, keeping his gaze on the page to give the widow a chance to calm herself. There was no body, that was the first problem. According to the peddler who'd brought the news, the Connecticut village had been so laid waste by the epidemic that all the dead had been thrown into one great pit. Nor were any proper records available, since the official responsible had been one of the first to die. "Inconvenient," Huddlestone murmured, "but the Court should take the circumstances into consideration."

"Court?" the widow repeated in fright.

"Mr. Gomez's will must be probated in the Prerogative Court, if the estate amounts to more than fifty pounds," he explained. "Unless he died intestate?"

She blinked again.

"Is there a will?" he spelled out gently.

"I suppose...there must be."

Huddlestone suppressed a sigh. Not that he liked the domineering sort of female—like that Dutch matron his father used to talk about, who'd called him in to draft a will for *herself*—but some of the ladylike ornaments of the present generation were as innocent as butterflies.

"I don't know what to do, sir," Mrs. Gomez said hoarsely, her milky fingernails half covering her mouth. "One hears such stories—widows mired in financial complications— jailed for debt, even!"

"Ah, but so great a merchant as your husband won't have left you exposed to danger."

She shuddered. "Without him—I feel entirely unprotected."

"Not entirely, I hope," said Huddlestone, allowing himself to touch his hand to his brocade waistcoat, in the general vicinity of his heart. Then he turned businesslike again. "Let me set your mind at rest, Mrs. Gomez; the laws of His Majesty's colony aren't as ungallant as you fear. Even without a will, you'll be entitled to a life interest in a third of the estate."

Her dark eyes were confused, and unconsoled.

"I can do nothing for your grief, madam, but perhaps I can banish your terrors—if you'll do me the honor of putting yourself quite in my hands?"

A moment's pause, and then she nodded, very fast.

Her naïveté charmed Huddlestone. His eyes rested on her

gold rings as he wondered how much he could get away with charging her.

That evening, over some hot chops he'd had sent up from the tavern, the attorney found himself savoring all the details he recalled of the young widow. Her tapered fingertips, protruding from her mittens; the intimate creak as she'd lifted her hoops when the interview was over. A sense of smooth, curved limbs under the layers of inky drapery. In response to his questions, she'd told him she'd been married at fourteen and boarded with her husband's family for the first few years. How these Jews kept their young on a tight rein! Huddlestone knew that his father was eager for grandsons, but at thirty-two he still hadn't found an appealing partner in life, and besides, he would rather hate to give up his bachelor liberties.

As he'd requested, Mrs. Gomez came back the very next day, her eyes shadowed by lack of sleep. She produced a sheaf of papers from a leather case. "I looked in his escritoire, as you advised, Mr. Huddlestone. I was obliged to smash the lock." She spoke breathlessly, as if she'd just committed a burglary.

"I'm sure your late husband would approve," he murmured, already leafing through the documents. "Mr. Gomez traded with Jamaica, I see?"

"And Barbados, and England, and many other places," she said. "I believe he imported dry goods and wine, and exported lumber and flour and such things."

I believe. Huddlestone suppressed a smirk; these fine damsels had no idea how their jewels and gowns got paid for. Ah, here was the will, as he'd hoped. The preamble was distinctively Semitic, to his ear: *I bequeath my Immortal Soul into the hands of the Almighty God of Israel...*

When he looked up, Mrs. Gomez was staring out the window onto Dock Street. "Have you read this, madam, may I ask?"

"Have I—"

He flushed; perhaps she'd never been taught. He knew Sephardics were an educated breed, but their females were a closed book to him. "Your husband's testament: has anyone told you its contents?"

"Oh, he did write one, then?"

Huddlestone grinned. "It's a rather extraordinary document, Mrs. Gomez. Composed, I venture to say, under the influence of sentiments most uxorious."

She blinked; perhaps she didn't know the word.

"It's a very simple document—ten times shorter than the typical will of a merchant." What Huddlestone didn't say was that in his experience, the average New York trader would prefer to chop off a finger than sign his name to such a thing. "Not only are you, his relict, named as sole executor, but also as..."—he paused in pleasurable suspense—"sole heir."

Her red mouth quivered. "I don't quite follow."

"Mr. Gomez's entire estate, after debts are paid, goes to you. Not just for your lifetime use, but outright!" The last time Huddlestone had seen such a will had been in the case of a vintner who'd turned out to have another wife and child back in England. He trusted there'd be no such hitches this time. "Not a penny is reserved for Mr. Gomez's kinsfolk or friends," he spelled out. In fact, for a Hebrew it was a particularly strange will; they usually left money to their unwed sisters, third cousins, congregation, even poor Jews back in Bohemia or the Barbados.

Mrs. Gomez still wasn't smiling.

"Madam," said Huddlestone, reaching across his bureau to seize her hand, "may I be the first to congratulate you on your great fortune?" She withdrew her fingers after a moment, and he wondered if he'd offended her. "How your late, lamented spouse must have doted on you," he rushed on. "And if I may say so, what a dazzling cornucopia of wifely virtues you must possess to be rewarded so richly in this time of mourning." *Shut up, man.*

The young widow was holding a handkerchief over her eyes. "Far from it."

"Come, madam—"

"I tried to perform my duty, that's all," she said, her voice thick with pain. "I have no special powers or talents; I make no pretence to wit. I ran his household, that's all." Her jaw moved as if she were grinding something between her teeth. "I gave him no heirs."

"Ah, but you gave him your youth," the attorney told her, and then realized how tactless that was. "The early part of it, I mean. You entrusted him with your obedient devotion, and in return he has bequeathed you his whole earthly estate."

The handkerchief came down, and the smoky eyes fixed on his. "What—what might it come to, sir?"

"Oh, you'll have to leave these papers with me before I

can put a figure to it," he told her. "But the estate appears to include substantial holdings in stocks and shares"—he leafed through the certificates—"as well as the house on Pearl Street, the blacks and other movables, and a part-interest in a ship..."

"Who knows what debts there may be, though?" Her face was still pinched with gloom. "But I suppose I must trust in the widow's cruse."

"The widow's cruse?" Huddlestone repeated, puzzled.

"A cruse, an earthenware jar," she hurried to explain. "From the story of Elisha and the widow. It refers to that pittance which can be eked out forever, by good management and God's grace."

"Ah, yes," he said, nodding, as if recalling the text.

After she'd gone, Huddlestone put his other tasks aside and spent the whole afternoon going through the Gomez papers.

Over a mug of cold punch and a pipe, that evening he reflected that the young widow was going to be a very great fortune indeed. She hardly seemed to realize it yet. She was all shrinking modesty; a true woman. She'd flinched at the prospect of thrusting herself into the public eye, by going to court to prove the will, which would involve confronting creditors, or any of the Gomez clan who might object to the wealth going out of the family. Huddlestone had had to assure her that he would guide and protect her, every step of the way.

He drew on his pipe, now, and mentally tripled the amount he was planning to bill her; she'd never know what other attorneys charged, and besides, it wasn't as if she couldn't spare it. He blessed the moment the heiress had stepped sideways into his little office, lifting her vast boned skirts. The tide of his fortune was turning, he could feel it; Huddlestone Junior was going to end up a richer man of the law than Huddlestone Senior had ever been. Mrs. Gomez was his luck, his good angel.

He sent his servant to the garret to poke around in a trunk for the Bible his father had given him as a boy. He found the story soon enough. The prophet Elisha told the debt-stricken widow to borrow empty jars from all her neighbors, and she kept pouring and pouring from her little cruse of oil until they were all filled up, which earned her enough to keep her in comfort for the rest of her days. Charmingly silly, thought Huddlestone.

Over the fortnight that followed, the attorney looked forward with growing excitement to Mrs. Gomez's daily visits. She blanched at the thought of probate dragging on for months—"I can't sleep, sir, I can't know a moment's peace until I've completed my duties as executor"—so he was doing everything possible to speed it up. He barked at one mulish court official: "How do you expect this poor widow to *produce the body* when it's moldering in a plague pit somewhere in the wilds of Connecticut?"

She'd relaxed with him, somewhat, he congratulated himself; it was like taming a sparrow. She now consented to a small glass of Madeira at each meeting. Making small talk, Huddlestone happened to mention the item in the *Weekly Journal* about the female pseudo-court that punished the violent husband. "No," said Mrs. Gomez, her head nunnishly on one side, "I cannot believe it of my sex."

"That's what I said to myself, madam."

"Women—if you'll permit a generalization—act more privately, more obscurely. According to the dictates of the heart." She spoke in a strangely bitter tone.

"Besides," he added pragmatically, "how would these creatures know enough to even mimic the correct procedures?"

Mrs. Gomez leaned slightly toward him. "Indeed. Consider my own case: I'm only too painfully aware that a woman alone, confronting the full weight and complexity of the law, might as well be lost in the bush at night."

"Ah, but what gentleman but would be only too happy to escort her home, with a lantern?" He'd got the gallant tone just right, Huddlestone considered, though he wasn't sure about the two *but*s.

There was some private darkness about her, he thought, lying awake that night; he couldn't quite put his finger on it. It wasn't just bereavement; he'd met many women who'd lost husbands, and they'd never had such complicated eyes.

"During marriage you were a nonperson, legally," he explained the next morning, "but now you're considered *feme sole* once more. You could even take up your husband's business, if his trading partners didn't object," he added playfully.

Mrs. Gomez sucked in her lips. "Oh, sir, I couldn't imagine anything more grueling. No"—her lovely face settled into fixed lines of sorrow again—"I don't even wish to maintain a household here."

"You'll sell your blacks, then?"

"I wish you to sell *everything* for me," she told him, with a new decisiveness. Was widowhood stiffening her backbone? "My husband's stocks, chattels, the house..."

"Very well. The proceeds could be put out at interest, to provide you with a guaranteed annuity."

She shook her head, little curls escaping from her cap at the temples. "I'd prefer the whole sum in gold, to take with me back to my father in Jamaica."

He frowned.

"I am always a foreigner here," she told him. "It is best to go, and the sooner, the better. To turn the page." She pressed her fingertips to her mouth as if she had said too much.

Somehow Huddlestone didn't like the idea of that glittering, winking fortune being carried off on a ship. It should stay in New York. Mrs. Gomez should stay, too.

That night he twisted in his sheets, irritated by the lumpy mattress. He relished his freedom, he reminded himself; what needs had he that servant and tavern and coffeehouse and laundry and (once in a while) a harlot picked up at the Battery couldn't meet? He'd never envied his married friends, with their snobbish wives and drooling infants. But Mrs. Gomez, with her dark lips and quivering lashes, her helplessness and her several thousand pounds...

By the time dawn broke over the East River, Huddlestone had made up his mind. This was his moment, he could taste it like spring on the air. *Nothing ventured,* as the proverb went.

When the Gomez business was done, instead of sending in his bill, he would present himself at the mansion in Pearl Street and ask for her hand.

His heart lurched in his ribcage. Although Huddlestone Senior might object to the lady's religion, the young attorney considered himself quite free of prejudice. Nor was the widow likely to turn him down on those grounds, since the supply of eligible bachelors in her tiny congregation could not be ample. How better, how much faster to *turn the page* than to take a new husband? Of course she'd felt like a foreigner, cooped up in that little nest of Caribbean Israelites. With an American husband—a bluff young attorney—her real life could begin.

A brief qualm struck him: the merchant had sired no children on her. But Huddlestone was sure he could do better; didn't her every curve seem to breathe ripeness? He reckoned it a positive advantage that she had experience of wifehood, she was like a well-broken horse. With her fortune— their fortune, he corrected himself, grinning in the dark— mightn't they take their place in the upper echelons of New York, alongside the great officials and landowners, and raise sons whose only trade was *gentleman?* He imagined a great canopied bed; guests sipping from cut crystal; sleigh rides to the Bowery.

The next day he felt as if he were suffering from a fever. Not scarlatina, he joked to himself, just love. His father, over Sunday dinner, accused him of a *coy expression*. Huddlestone drank too much at night; by day, he neglected all other business but the Gomez estate. He brought the will's

witnesses into court, harried debtors, and organized a public
vendue to turn the contents of the house on Pearl Street into
cash. (It seemed a shame to part with the handsome, heavy
furniture and silverware, he thought, but this way, the newly-
weds could begin afresh, with everything in the latest style.)
Huddlestone worked with a thorough zeal that was strange
to him, and all the while the image of Mrs. Gomez floated in
front of his eyes. She might wear pale blue to their wedding;
she might wear lilac. Oddly enough, he thought he liked her
best in black.

When the great day came, and Huddlestone arrived at the
almost empty mansion with two strong men carrying a trunk
full of gold, Mrs. Gomez let out a little cry.

"Not a penny more than you merit, madam. May I congratulate you," he asked, "on bearing up so bravely, these
weeks past?"

She shook her head as if overcome.

He inquired gently whether there would be a funeral.

"Oh, yes," she assured him, "I mean to do all that money
can."

This casual reference to the trunkful of gold made Huddlestone's stomach twist. Did she not realize that a really
splendid funeral, with a hired *inviter* and barrels of wine and
tobacco, commemorative gloves and scarves and rings for all
the mourners, could cost several hundred pounds? "May I
offer a word of counsel, Mrs. Gomez? The governor looks
askance at the fashion for extravagant funerals. In the absence of a body, in particular, it might seem improper..."

She hadn't thought of that; perhaps he was right.

"Of course, whatever form the obsequies may take, I need hardly tell you that I shall be present as—if you'll permit—your advisor, your prop, your staff."

"Oh, Mr. Huddlestone." A wet glitter in her eyes. "Such excess of kindness—lavished on an undeserving woman—"

"Nonsense!" What could explain that air of sorrowful mystery about the young widow? he wondered. What could have infused such infinite regret into that perfect face? He longed to understand it almost more than to wipe it away.

"These past weeks—"

"The pleasure has been very great. And all mine," he said incoherently.

"I can only say how sorry I am for all the trouble to which I've put you."

He was briefly speechless; his arms made a circling motion as if to say that all that he was, all that he could do, was at her feet.

"You must be sure to send in your bill promptly," she reminded him in a whisper as the servant came to show him out.

The days that followed were full of pleasurable anticipations, and the nights brought scalding dreams. His sheets were dreadfully stained; he had to send them out for laundering. His best silk suit was aired and brushed, ready for the funeral. Perhaps he would act directly afterwards, while the widow was at her most vulnerable. He mulled over the wording. He tried out every variation, from *May I be so bold as to make a proposal which may be of mutual benefit,* to *I insist that you be mine.*

Huddlestone was in his window seat at the coffeehouse when his eye was caught by the name.

One Mr. Gomez, a merchant, given out for dead of the scarlatina, yesterday arrived in New York, perfectly well, to the astonishment of his family.

He gripped the paper so hard, it tore. The coffee turned to bile in his mouth. He'd come so close, his fortunes had trembled on the verge of transformation. . . . To hell with this Lazarus, and to hell with Connecticut peddlers for reporting rumor as truth!

How ecstatic Mrs. Gomez would be this morning. Would she throw off her weeds at once and appear in white swanskin and taffeta? It was like a Bible story: all her wifely grief rewarded by this miraculous resurrection. If she'd ever felt anything for her attorney—a mild trust, at most, Huddlestone thought in humiliation—it was nothing compared to her wifely fervor.

Just wait till they see my bill!

Out in the street, the air stank; somebody had to be burning oyster shells. Huddlestone talked himself from rage to mere gloom. What kind of demon was he, to begrudge the woman her newfound bliss? After all, she'd never given him any open encouragement, promised him nothing. Wasn't it her melancholic modesty, her shrinking from any selfish desire, that had attracted him? *Come, man, it's nobody's fault.*

Perhaps he would pay a call. His feet were already taking him toward Pearl Street. It was common decency to congratulate the widow-turned-wife, to wish the happy couple well. (But he would leave it to some other attorney to sort out their legal muddle.) He would drop by only briefly, to take one last glimpse of that scarlet, startled mouth.

At Pearl Street the manservant annoyed him by insisting that his mistress was gone abroad. "I think you mean," said Huddlestone, "that she *intended* to go back to her family in Jamaica. But under the circumstances—"

No, the fellow wouldn't budge; Mrs. Gomez had shipped out of New York a week ago, she'd missed the master's return by a matter of days. Would the visitor like to speak to the master?

Huddlestone shook his head hurriedly; it occurred to him for the first time that Gomez might see him as having been culpably negligent, to rush through the probating of the will without a proper proof of death.

His head was throbbing with confusion. Down by the docks, he interrogated some sailors, to disprove the servant's ridiculous story. Just as he thought, there'd been no ships embarking for Jamaica in the past fortnight. The only sailings had been to Liverpool, Rotterdam, Lisbon, and the Cape. Besides, why would Mrs. Gomez have left New York in such a scramble, before the funeral, with the house not yet sold, without saying a word to her attorney? By what sickening stroke of ill luck could she have just missed being reunited with her husband?

It was only then, his eyes on the choppy waters of the East River, his nostrils full of the stench of fish, that Huddlestone woke, as if he'd been slapped. It came to him that he'd been a sleepwalker, tangled in the kind of muddy dream in which, while it lasts, monstrosities make sense. *Of course, of course.*

Why, a halfwit of thirteen could have seen through Mrs. Gomez's performance! The signs shone out now as if carved on the pale gray sky over the harbor. The missing corpse; the unavailable documents. *Oh, he did write a will?* The shows of ignorance. *I'd prefer the whole sum in gold.* The pleas for urgency. *To turn the page.* She'd appealed to Huddlestone's vanity, and to his gallantry. His avarice. His sweaty dreams.

He walked back up Dock Street like a frail old man, jostled by the crowd. She'd practically waved the truth in his face: *The sooner the better. I mean to do all that money can.* Why had the Jewess played such a terrible trick on her husband, he wondered dizzily? Had Gomez been miserly, malicious, a brute? *I tried to perform my duty,* she said coolly in Huddlestone's head, *I ran his household. We were not so blessed.* What could the merchant have done to deserve being robbed of his whole life's estate?

The strange thing was, it struck him, the will had been dated only last year. Could adoration have gone septic so fast? What was the hard black cherry pit at the core of their marriage?

Unless she'd forged the document, somehow. It struck Huddlestone that he'd underestimated the education of Sephardic girls. Those two taciturn men who'd testified in court that they'd seen Gomez sign the will, could they have been her accomplices? Her lovers? His imagination reeled.

Most likely he would never know. But of course he didn't really care about her treachery to Gomez. She'd betrayed Huddlestone, her husband-who-might-have-been, when he'd only meant to help her. She'd robbed three weeks from his life, but it felt as if he'd been in her thrall forever. *Women act more privately, more obscurely,* she'd remarked. *According to the dictates of the heart.* Was that a coded warning? *Such excess of kindness—lavished on an undeserving woman.* Had she been laughing at him all along, or had there been some true regret mixed in with the fake? *I can't sleep, sir,* she'd told him, *I can't find any peace. I can only say how sorry I am for all the trouble to which I've put you.* Such sad eyes. He needed to believe one line at least, a single shard saved from the wreckage.

He would always be puzzling now, always doubting. Never understanding the real story. Liverpool, Rotterdam, Lisbon, the Cape? Never knowing where in the world she'd gone.

As Huddlestone mounted the stairs to his apartment, and let himself fall onto his bed, it came to him that he would live and die a bachelor.

The Widow's Cruse

We hear that the wife of a certain Merchant of this city, while her husband was in the country, broke open his scrutore, and took out his will, of which she was executrix; and went in widow's weeds to Doctor's Commons, under a pretence that he was dead, and prov'd the same; by virtue whereof she receiv'd all his money in the stocks, and is gone over sea.

New York Weekly Journal (May 26, 1735)

This intriguing sentence was preserved by Carol Berkin and Leslie Horowitz in their *Women's Voices, Women's Lives: Documents in Early American History* (1998). Huddlestone and Mrs. Gomez are fictional members of two real New York families, bottom-drawer lawyers and Sephardic merchants respectively.

TEXAS
1864

LAST SUPPER AT BROWN'S

Before the War there's two women in the house but last year Marse done took them to auction. Now's just me, the cook and all-round boy. My name Nigger Brown, I don't got no other, I was born here.

Missus done came in the kitchen this morning, unlock the butter barrel. *Law,* she say, *that'll be gone in a week.*

She don't call me boy, like Marse do. She don't call me nothing. She only marry Brown a couple years back, too late for chillun. Some say hims took her for the money from her laundry but she ain't ugly, I done seen worse. I say, *Maybe I make you some ash cakes?*

Ash cakes, are they colored fixings?

I tells her, *Taste real fine. All's I need is meal, water, pinch of lard.*

Missus smile, almost. *Very good. How much flour's left?*

Less 'n a barrel.

She jangling her keys like a rattle. She know she ain't quality, she still got laundress hands. She come down to lock and unlock her stores before most every meal, sometime I reckon she come to the kitchen just so's not to be upstairs with Marse. Same thing, she work the garden with her India

65

rubber gloves on, I's a-digging and a-toting and a-watering, days pass. We'uns don't talk much, we'uns know what we doing.

She open the sugar cupboard, now, there ain't so much as a hogshead full.

Can't you order some more, ma'am? I says.

Her breath hiss. *I'm afraid the store won't allow us another thing, with times as they are.*

Since the blockade, no cotton's getting shipped out, port's quiet like a cemetery. I hear Marse at dinner sometime boasting the damn Yankees ain't got into none of Texas yet and never will. He sing out, *This here's the last frontier.* Planters coming down from Georgia and Virginia with all thems darkies to make a stand.

How much coffee's left? ask Missus now.

Half a sack.

She give a long sigh.

In these parts four out of five is colored. The buckras, they's always sniffing out plots among their blacks but there ain't no trouble in this part of Texas. We'uns just waiting the War out. Passing on what stories we hear tell, sitting tight.

For dinner I roast the last of the gobblers, with ash cakes and corn and the end of the catsup.

Afterwards I's eating leftovers in the kitchen. Missus come in and start counting the preserves. *He means to ride to town with you tomorrow.*

That so?

You know why?

No, Ma'am.

Guess, she say, like playing with a chile. I can see her teeth but she ain't smiling. I shake my head. *Guess,* she say again.

My collar feel real tight. I been in this house since I was born. *Marse won't do that.*

Some might call that back talk but Missus like a straight answer. She come up close, her fingers all tangled. *I tell you, I've been married to Brown five years come June, and there's nothing he wouldn't do.*

He mean to sell me?

The man said to me just now, That nigger buck's worth a thousand dollars. She lean on the table. *Don't you see? You're all he's got left.*

I think I might fall down.

He intends to leave you with a dealer in town tomorrow, buy some calves instead.

That ain't gone happen. I says it real quiet but I know she hear me.

Missus nod.

Mary? That's Marse a-shouting for her. She shoot off like a rabbit.

I got a lot to do. I find some old bags in the larder, start filling them. Cornmeal, flour, salt pork mostly. A couple handful of coffee for when I need to stay wake. The littlest pot for boiling.

Missus come back in so quiet I don't hear her till she touch my elbow, and I jump. She don't wear no clickety-clackety heels like other missuses. Too late to hide what I'm doing. She could call in Marse and have me whupped for thieving right this minute.

Take this, she whisper, holding up a jar of peaches.

I shake my head. *It get broke,* I tell her.

She set it down, unlock the sugar cupboard, start a scooping. *Where do you plan to run?*

Now here's where I reckon I should seal up my mouth, but Missus, she already done got the noose round my neck. *Mexico, I reckon,* I says, real soft, *or the Arizona Territory.*

I'm coming, she say. Like she was talking about a party.

My face is stony. *Missus Brown—*

That's not my real name, she remark. *I'm only called Brown the same way you are, because of him.* She jerk her head upstairs, where Marse's lying on his'n couch with his'n bottle.

Missus, you talking crazy. You can't come nowhere along of me.

Well I can't stay with him, she mutter, still a-scooping the sugar. *If I stay in this house another month—*

Listen, I start.

I'll pick up this knife and put an end to it, she say. Her hand be on the handle, skin on bone.

What this man done to her? I look in her brown eyes. *You slow me down,* I says, *I gotta move fast. I be a stray buck, contraband.*

She smiling now, strange. *But I know how to sign for him, you see, I've practiced. I can sign a travel pass for you with my husband's name! We'll go in the carriage, and if patrollers stop us, I'll say I'm going to visit my family.*

I wants to shake her real hard. *You think Marse won't lep*

up, soon's he find his bed empty, ride over to Stern's planta-tion and put the alarm out?

She chewing on her lip.

They come for us with dogs. They come with irons.

Damn you, she say, eyes shining wet, *I can't—* She turn round, she gone into the house.

On my own in the kitchen I gets a-thinking. She ain't bad, for a white woman. I wouldn't much mind her com-ing along. Like she say, take the carriage, show a pass, get farther faster that way. If it wasn't impossible, it be a good plan.

My mind a-hopping about like a fly. If she could sneak out in the night without Marse knowing. If he sleep long, sleep all night and all day—but no, we'uns need more of a head start than that.

Halfway through the afternoon Missus come in again. Her eyes red but she got a hold of herself.

About supper, I says, before she speak a word.

I don't give a damn about supper.

I takes a breath, I says, *You don't care for okra, do you?* I don't say Missus.

She shrug.

Okra. It not your favorite.

Well, no. My favorite would be sweet potato, she say, *the way you fix it with molasses.*

I be sure to fix some sweet potato tonight, just for you.

Do, if you like, say Missus, like some girl.

You be eating that sweet potato instead of that okra.

She look at me again, hard.

Since you don't care for okra. Specially not the way I's fixing it tonight.

She don't say nothing.

I can't be sure. I don't know how much to tell her. *Marse gonna like it, though. Eat hims fill, bet you he does.*

She take a step over to me. *What's in the okra?*

Never you mind, I tell her. *I's the cook. Yeah?*

I suppose.

So leave the cooking to me.

When she gone I get the rest of supper all fixed and then I make the okra. My heart a-going boom-boom. I's never made it till now but I know how, my pappy teach me. I done pick the stuff in the woods months back, it be always in my charm bag round my neck. There come a moment I feel bad, but I says to myself, *Marse mean to leave you with this dealer tomorrow, buy some calves.* I taste the okra, just touch it to my tongue to be sure, then stir in more sugar. Marse, he like hims fixings sweet.

I bring in the supper like always. While they eating I wait outside. I think I hear talking, dishes and lids, plates and glasses. After while I don't hear nothing. Not a word, not a holler. That's worse. I wait.

This the moment. This's it. I feels like some blind man. This the time my life split like a peach, and there's a rotten side and a sweet yellow side, and which it gonna be?

Missus come out. Mary, that her name. I think maybe she gonna scream murder after all. Did we'uns understand each our selves? Did she think hims only going sleep? Or maybe she scared, now it come to it, maybe she say *Go.*

Instead she put her hand in mine, real cool, smooth. No speaking.

I follow her into the room where Marse lie facedown in the okra. We stand for a little, make sure he not moving none.

Should I clear away? I ask, not sure what I mean, except to get him out of sight.

Missus shake her head. *Never mind that.*

It should be three, four day before any neighbor think to ride over to Brown's. Maybe a week. He not a social man.

She turn, look in my face, she say, *I packed my bag.* Her hand like a knot in mine.

Last Supper at Brown's

A clipping from the *Tucson Star,* pasted in Scrapbook No. 1 at the Sharlot Hall Museum in Prescott, Arizona, records that Negro Brown, aka Nigger Brown, killed his master in Texas in 1864 and "throughout all his wanderings...he was accompanied by his slain master's wife."

Susan Johnson, in "Sharing Bed and Board: Cohabitation and Cultural Difference in Central Arizona Mining Towns, 1863–1873" (in *The Women's West,* edited by Susan Armitage and Elizabeth Jameson, 1987), rounds up various newspaper accounts that suggest the wife in question was Mary Brown, aka Mary DeCrow. The runaways' romance seems to have lasted no longer than the journey into Arizona. That state's 1864 census lists "Negro Brown" as living with "Santa Lopez" and a baby, and "Mary Brown," a forty-two-year-old laundress from Texas, as living with a twenty-nine-year-old Mexican blacksmith called Cornelius Ramos (or Ramez or Reamis). She married Ramos the following year; they ran a boardinghouse, then worked mining claims and set up a goat ranch.

IN TRANSIT

GULF OF SAINT LAWRENCE
1849

COUNTING THE DAYS

Jane Johnson grips the rail of the *Riverdale*, watching the estuary water heave and sink below her. She reckons the dates: nearly five weeks since she boarded at Belfast, and the city of Québec is only one more day west. The provisions might almost have lasted, if it hadn't been for the heat and the maggots in the ham. The same journey took Henry eight weeks last year, when the seas were high. Tomorrow she will be beside him.

Today she is beside herself. On this voyage Jane has discovered herself to be a most imperfect creature. For all her weather-dried red hair and her two children, she is restless as a young goat that butts the fence. What has appalled her the most on this little floating world of the *Riverdale* is not the squalor, nor the hunger, but the dearth of news. No one has left their company, except for that old man who died of dysentery last week. No one has arrived, unless you count a stillbirth down in steerage. The only gossip is the rumble of clouds and the occasional protest of gulls. The passengers have to spend their time guessing what is happening in the real, landlocked world, now split in two for them like an apple, where on one side people weep for them and stare into the horizon that has swallowed them up, and on the other side, others stare back, waiting for the first glimpse of them. Or at least so these passengers must believe. Unless they are longed for, why are they here, cribbed in the rancid belly of this wooden whale?

Jane reaches into her pocket for her cache of letters and loosens the ribbon. They're too few: crumbs to her appetite. The first, bearing the postmark, Henry didn't send till he'd been there a fortnight. He wanted to wait till he had good news to tell, *something encouraging,* he wrote, the eejit, as if she needed any message but his living scribble on the paper, between the edges that are black from a month crossing the Atlantic to her.

Henry Johnson leans against a wall in Montréal. *I am thinking great long to see you,* his wife says at various points in the creased pages. Her grammar makes him want to slap her, and take her in his arms, and cry.

He should be in the shop, helping with the dinnertime customers, but he had to step out to get a little air. Maybe the sunlight and the long shadows of the trees will settle him. Maybe he is just nervous because of the trip he must take tonight, down the sinewy St. Lawrence to Québec. When he gets back, at the end of the week, it will be with Jane and the little ones: he will be a family man once more.

Dear Henry when you and me meet we will have many an old story to tell each other.

Such weakness is slackening his limbs today. His stomach churns; he leans against the wall. Its timber frame bears the claw marks of last winter's ice. A carriage clatters by; the crack of the whip rings in Henry's ears. His nerves are spiders' webs beneath his skin. Have the months of vagabonding and working hand to mouth taken such a toll? Henry is an older man than the brash grocer who fled Antrim and debts last year. But a stronger one, surely. The bad times are over; he is going to be the husband Jane has always deserved.

She clambered onto the ship at the warm end of May, with Alex behind her, small fists full of her skirt, and Mary heavy on her hip. By the first week in June, the air had thickened. Jane had begged from everyone who shared any of her names to make up the twenty pounds for this cabin. She and the children are sharing it with two aged clergymen. The air is fetid, but anything is better than Antrim. At least on ship she doesn't have to jam the door against whoever might knock.

In such a famine year it is better not to think about home. The town of Antrim has lidded its eyes. Most of those who are not dead have been evicted; the rest count farthings or starve in private. What overwhelms Jane, when she lets herself dwell on it, is the sense of anticlimax: the Johnsons held themselves together through four years of blight, but where is their happy-ever-after?

Down in the steaming gloom of the cabin, she hunches on the bunk with her eyes squeezed shut, and tries to find her better self. At least they have some bedding, not like some of the passengers, who sleep in the spare sails. Besides, what right has she to make a fuss about leaving for a faraway country when her uncle did it years before her, and her nephew, and her brother, and her two sisters? And her husband. Against her better judgment she let Henry go on ahead;

thirteen months without anyone to wash his shirt. What kind of wife is she? She jolts the crying girl on her lap, watching dark water punch the glass circle. What kind of a woman would be more loath to go than to part, more afraid of the crossing than the separation?

Sometimes Henry's letters are so obstinately cheerful that they hurt her throat. *I have had rather a rough time of it,* he remarked after the storm off Liverpool. The paper was stiff with salt; the water had spewed in and nearly sunk the ship. Is his bravery a fiction, Jane sometimes wonders? When he wrote to assure her that he had not panicked like the papists who threw holy water on the waves, was it her or himself he was trying to convince? *I knew if we were to go down I might as well take it Kindly as not as crying wouldnt help me.*

They all think him a cheerful character: the other fellows in the shop, his Frenchie landlady, and before that, the farmers he lodged with in exchange for kitchen work, down by the Great Falls. Henry Johnson cultivates a reputation for cheer. The way he sees it, it is only civil to Providence to seem grateful.

It would surprise him to be told that he is eaten up with anger. Or rather, that anger serves Henry, devours whatever stands in his way: tiredness, inertia, despair, and loneliness. Plowing though six-foot snowdrifts, anger has burned in his gut and kept him warm, or warm enough to keep walking anyway.

Henry credits Providence with bringing him so far, but it could be that it was anger that did it, anger that dragged him away from Antrim in the first place. Anger has carried him halfway across the world; he hopes to seed a little patch of the soil of this vast country with it.

Something is burning in his guts now. His fingertips ache; he presses them against the wall outside the shop where he should be serving customers. He fixes his thoughts on Jane; everything will be ordinary again the minute she disembarks. Lying in Carrickfergus gaol, he used to conjure her up in the shadows: her stiff apron, her sandy hair coming out of its net, her huge laugh. *Dear Henery. I hope your not reflecting on the past but always looking forward.*

His letters make casual mention of *six weeks walk* and *five hundred miles*. Some of the places he writes of or from have a familiar ring—Lucan, Hamilton, New London, where Jane's sisters are—but others are like strange fruit in her mouth: Niagara, Montréal. Québec is her destination, but she had no idea how to pronounce it until she asked the clergyman on the opposite bunk. All she knows of this new world is words scattered on a page.

The river is beginning to narrow around the ship. Jane stares at the green hills, the fields dotted with cottages and the occasional spire that hooks the light. *I felt almost as if I was getting home again,* Henry wrote in an early letter. But other times the strangeness of the place shows through his lines. He speaks of vast waterfalls, Indians, juice leaking from the trees. He assures her they need bow to no one in this country: *The Servant eats at the Same table with his master.* But on the outside of one envelope he scrawls, *Bring the gun.*

The afternoon has dimmed around him and still Henry

cannot move from the back wall. He has never felt this queasy since the days when he used to be a drinker.

There is doubt in his wife's letters, tucked between the lines of devotion. Jane reports that his mother hopes he will come back to the old country; that her parents advise her not to make the crossing yet; that she only wishes he had found a permanent job and could send money. She offers with one hand and takes back with the other. *If you fall into your mind and would wish me to go to you I will, let the end be what it may.*

He turns and is sick into a bush. Its dark leaves quiver. Some foreign species; he doesn't know its name.

Wringing out the children's rags in a bucket of seawater, Jane tries to imagine the country ahead of her. The ship sways, and brown water slops from the bucket onto her skirt. She wants to howl. But she will go up on deck and let it dry in the sun, then brush the worst of it out. She has no time to be weak. She is resolved not to be a burden. What is she bringing Henry, if not a capacity for endurance?

The hard fact is, she needs him more than he needs her. For the past year, he has been an adventurer; she has been paralyzed, a wife without a husband. Sometimes she hates Henry for going on ahead, for being able and willing to do without her in a strange land. But this is how Jane knows her kin, by an occasional flash of a resentment so intimate that she never feels it for outsiders: the maddening itch of the ties that bind.

Henry wipes his sour mouth on the handkerchief Jane embroidered for him two Christmases ago. He leafs through the worn letters for some magic phrase to calm him. But what his eyes light on is *You might write to me far oftener than you do.* Can she imagine what it is like to be here so many thousand miles from home, with no one to offer him a cup of tea or a word of sympathy?

The hard fact is, he needs her more than she needs him. He suspects Jane of enjoying her new independence; more and more, she writes to him after making decisions, not before. Anger swells in his throat now; he can taste gall all the way down. But he recognizes this rage as a symptom of distance, the lengths love has to go to, the tautness of a marriage stretched like a tendon across a wide ocean. It costs them one and fourpence, paid in advance, to send each page.

The children are clamoring for some biscuit, despite the weevils. She has none, but she tells herself it will not kill them to wait just one more day. Jane squats down and holds them tightly round their waists, as if to squeeze the hunger pangs away. Alex and Mary both have her pale red hair; their three heads like a litter of foxes.

Across the deck she sees those two women who came on at Liverpool, clinging to each other mutely as if they expect to be washed overboard at any moment. One of them bends over the water to be sick; the other one waits with a cloth to wipe her mouth. Jane envies them each other. She is so weary of the feel of children, even her own beloved children; she wants a shoulder high enough to lean on, arms as hard as her own.

Henry has told his boss he is too sick to work, and now he is trying to walk back to his lodgings. He bends and retches onto the dusty ground as if voiding himself of thirteen months of self-pity. A passing lady withdraws her skirts. A priest tells him, in broken English, to go home. Henry is too weak to answer. He lets his head hang, and skims Jane's letters through blurred eyes.

Excuse bad writing and inditing, she wrote, as if every word were not a gift.

Henry averts his face from the page and throws up again, though there is little left but bitter air. If he purges himself of all his past errors, maybe there will be space for happiness to come flooding in.

His bowels have begun to churn. He tries to run. When shit sprays into his breeches and he doubles over, he is ashamed. But no one is paying him any attention; those who rush by are on business of their own. The streets are beginning to darken. Henry tucks the letters into his shirt and pulls his braces and trousers down, squatting to empty his bowels on the cracked ground. Pain spears him: the dark water keeps exploding. His solid flesh has become a bag of filth.

At some point he fastens up his trousers for decency, for some kind of containment, and staggers down the street. But the cramps bend him in two, like low blows from an invisible enemy.

Twilight finds him lying in a puddle of his own fluids, too weak to excuse himself when a woman stoops over him. She backs away, shouting something in French. He thinks he recognizes the word for anger. Who is angry? Then the woman shouts it again, and he recognizes the word like his own name.

As the light fades, Alex chatters of hunters and bears; Mary kicks at the railings and wriggles as if she wants to slip through into the sea. *You and them has never once been out of my mind and heart since I left you:* that is from Jane's favorite of the letters. She has taught the girl to say *Dida*, the first name Jane knew for her own father. Mary has no idea what the word means, and plays with the sound as a bird would. Neither child is old enough to understand that they have left the only country they have ever known, to settle in a new one. They will be Canadians; Jane mouths the word to herself. It is not a matter of choice. What choice have any of them made, when all they know is what they are running from, when Henry with his exasperating enthusiasm is leading them into the dark?

Cholera, that's what the woman said. Henry nods slightly. He is folded into a hospital bed like a leaf pressed in a book. The diarrhea is finished, and so is the vomiting; he has nothing left to offer up. He has given every drop in his body to this alien soil.

Cholera, anger made flesh, the dull burning fuse in the guts, the bile spewing through the bodies of those who stay and those who go. A disease familiar to those who are herded from country to country, from city to city.

This ward is filling up; the nurses run like messengers bearing secrets. Each new arrival is doled out forty drops of laudanum. Henry can tell, by looking at the cadaverous faces around him, that his cheeks are concave, his eyeballs are sinking in their sockets, and he too has taken on a blue tinge, as if they are all part of the same boiling sea.

He closes his eyes. He shuts his ears to the moans and retchings and convulsions all around him. In his mind, he reads fragments of letters. *Our best Days are before us.*

It occurs to him for the first time that he may be dying.

He knows he should pray. His God is unsentimental; he sits in judgment. There is no time left for Henry's old prayer, the one he directs as much at his wife as at his Creator: *make me what I have not been yet, a good and providing husband.*

At dawn on the day of arrival, Jane is up on deck again. The *Riverdale* has come to an enticing green island, its slopes furred with beech and ash; blue strings of smoke rise from the sheds. Grosse Isle is its name, she hears; it is where the sick must disembark. The ship pauses only long enough to set down the two gray-faced women from Liverpool. Jane watches their little boat bob toward the shore, with as much relief as compassion.

The sun is high by the time she glimpses the walled city of Québec on the promontory, pushing into the river like a sentry's gun. The fiction on which she has lived for a year is about to come true. At the sight of its towers, Jane lets out a small moan. Has she not been brave long enough?

Soon Henry will be walking beside her, lifting the children to his shoulders, pointing out landmarks. He will make up to her for all the waiting. She leafs through the letters, hungry for a sentence she remembers, the sweetness of his admission that they should never have let themselves be parted, *but dont be discouraged Dear Jane.*

This morning for the first time she lets herself taste how hungry she is, lets the children see her cry. But she shakes back the tears so she can glimpse the busy docks, the ladders that will set the passengers free from their prison.

Henry floats up from unconsciousness and wonders what Jane will do when she steps off the ship and he is not there. *P.S. Dear Henry do not neglect to meet us.* Which will win out, her panic or her anger? There is no letter he can write to tell her the end of the story. She will have to deduce it from his absence, interpret the suspicion in the faces of the French on the quay, read death in the yellow flags that mark the medicine stations.

Where will she go? Surely the Emigration Agent will take pity and pay her way to New London. Henry prays his wife will come safe through the plains shaking with heat, the summer storms, the waist-deep mud of Toronto, and reach her sisters before the winter and a cold like she has never known. How long before she hears for sure that she is a widow at twenty-six? Until then, will she keep writing letters? he wonders. No, Jane is a practical woman; she would not write without an address. That is how he picked her: as a fellow traveler in a whirling world, a rock in a hard place.

Leaning over the rails, Jane imagines the improvement; that slightly hunted look will be gone from her husband's face. What a cocky letter he sent recently: *I am 14 lbs heavier than I was when I left and I Can go into the bush and chop a log.* But so much will be the same: his dark eyes, his sweep of hair, the way his hands will close around hers.

Maybe he will have brought some food with him.

How will she live, Henry speculates through his fog of fever? Will she and her sisters go into trade together? Or will she find some slow-moving neighbor to take on her and the children, some Irishman twice her age who will be husband and father both?

Will she still count the days she has to live without Henry in this country?

He will be there on the dock, for sure. *Without you I will settle myself no place,* he wrote in the letter that persuaded Jane to come at once, not to wait a month more, because you never knew what might happen. *And Jane Dearest anything I can do Shall be done to make you happy and forgive anything wrong in the foregoing.* Every letter is a promise, signed and sealed; they all end, *your faithful and affectionate husband until death.*

His skin is cold and wet like a fish; the only water left in his body is on the outside. Henry licks his shoulder. He is sinking down below all human things. He is sliding into the ocean; he will not wait till her ship meets the land. He will sport around it like a dolphin, he will make her laugh louder than the gulls.

He shuts his eyes and swims down into the darkness.

Jane peers at the landing stage where the crowds are milling. That speck of black, standing so still, that must be him. His eyes, sharper than hers, will have marked her out already. What distances cannot be traveled by the gaze of love?

Counting the Days

All italicized lines are taken verbatim from the thirteen letters (May 1848–May 1849) between Henry Johnson and Jane McConnell Johnson published by their great-granddaughter Louise Wyatt in *Ontario History* (1948). You can find more details about the family in Wyatt's introduction to the letters at http://ied.dippam.ac.uk/records/49618.

On landing in July 1849—and not finding Henry—Jane and the children went on to her sister Isabella's in London, Ontario. Confirmation of her husband's death from cholera did not reach her for three months. Within a year, Jane married a local farmer of fifty-three, William Nettleton from Belfast; they had seven more children.

THE YUKON
1896

SNOWBLIND

They were both heading for the Yukon goldfields when they ran into each other in St. Michael, the old Russian port on the Alaskan coast. Goat (named for his yellow goatee) was a Swede, and Injun Joe was from Iowa; folk said Injun looked more than half Indian but he didn't know if it was true. They'd both turned twenty-two that July, and it was this coincidence that convinced them to hitch up. It has to mean luck, said Goat, doesn't it? It had to mean something.

Both of them had put their hands to just about anything since hard times got harder round 'ninety-three. Injun had been an apple picker, a ranch hand, a slaughterman; he'd even done a few prizefights till an Irish boy blinded his left eye. Goat had played three-card monte and thrown drunks out of a whorehouse. They were both tough as hardtack, could tote seventy pounds, and scorned a quitter. Neither knew much about prospecting except that it was all they wanted to do. Goat said he was "gold crazy," was that the phrase? It'd only been a few years since he'd come from Sweden with eighty-five cents in his pocket. His English was good but he didn't trust it. He claimed he'd take a fifteen-dollar poke of gold dust over a twenty-dollar banknote, he was sentimental that way, he just loved the sparkle of it.

After paying for the boat ride up the Yukon, the two fellows were down to their sleeping bags, tent, and seven-odd dollars between them. But at least they'd found each other. You'd got to have a partner or you wouldn't make it, that's what the old-timers said. It wasn't just that so much of gold mining took four hands, it was the risk of going off your head in the dark of winter. In Fortymile—the shack town just over the border into Canadian territory, where the two got off because Goat was sick of the tug of the boat against the current—they met a grizzled sourdough with six missing toes. He'd had a split-up back in 'eighty-six, the two had divided their outfit fair and square, and the toeless man had left his former mate to work the claim. It was a whipsaw that did it, he said, whipsawing green logs put paid to many a friendship, because you got in a rage and couldn't trust the other fellow was pulling his weight.

The old sourdough asked Injun Joe if he was one of those lazy Stick Indians from the interior. Injun shook his head and said I'm from Iowa. Truth was, he would have liked knowing what he was or where he was from on his father's side; his mother (pure Pole) had never said, and he'd stopped asking long ago.

Fortymile was more of a camp than any kind of town—it looked like a heap of garbage washed up on the riverbank— but Injun reckoned it had all they needed, for now. Since every man in sight was a prospector, whether a veteran of Dakota, Idaho, or Colorado, or a tenderfoot like Goat and

Injun, it was like being in a gang. A gang of loners, if such a thing could be. *Outside,* that was what they called everything outside Fortymile.

McQuesten, the storeowner, never refused credit; he boasted that no one ever starved to death here, or not unless he was too stupid to roll from his bunk and crawl into town. Injun and Goat were able to outfit themselves at McQuesten's on a promise of payback come spring. They kitted themselves out in gumboots, mackinaws, mukluks, and the broad-brimmed hats that kept off rock splinters. (After all, Injun was down to one useful eye already.) They filled a wheelbarrow with kerosene lamps, a panning tank, a stew kettle, a saw, and a couple of short-stemmed shovels, tin plates and forks, rope and coal oil, beans, cornmeal, baking powder, lard, salt, chocolate, and tea, and on top, a fragile-looking copper scales and a phial of mercury wrapped in a handkerchief. This mountain of gear was too precarious to wheel around the wilderness, so they left most of it in the back of McQuesten's while they went off prospecting along the creeks of the Fortymile.

They'd pick a likely spot, spit in the can for luck, let the water wash away the mud, and peer into the bottom for the glitter. The first time they found some it had a startling greenish tinge to it. Injun let out a yelp like an injured dog, and Goat got him in a half nelson and kissed his ear.

This was why the Yukon was the place to be, even if there hadn't been any real big strikes yet. In some goldfields, the stuff was veined into the hard rock, and only expensive machinery could blast it out, but the Yukon gave up her treasure casually to any man who took the trouble to look for it. Placer gold—free gold, some called it—lying around in the white gravel in the form of good coarse dust or nuggets even. This first spot gave five cents' worth of gold dust from the pan, when Injun weighed it with slightly shaking hands. The toeless fellow reckoned eight cents a pan's a pretty good prospect, he said, but Goat laughed and said this here looked pretty good to him. He wanted to stake their claim right away; Injun had to talk him into waiting to see if they could find a richer spot. (In Fortymile, Injun had got the impression Swedes were pitied for their willingness to stake a prospect other men would dig a shit pit on.)

At night the two fellows lay back-to-back in their sailcloth tent, and in the mornings they counted their bruises; the man with the fewest had to boil the coffee. That was their first game but soon they had plenty. After another week they found a bend in a muddy creek that gave ten cents a pan, and Injun felt the glow of being right, as well as the giddy antic- ipation of riches. Goat marked out the five hundred feet he liked best; Injun blazed a small spruce tree and penciled on the upstream side, *One,* and their names.

That night they lay awake so long laughing and planning how to spend their fortune, they were baggy-eyed when they hiked into Fortymile to the Recorder's Office. The two of them were so ignorant, they hadn't realized that they were allowed a claim each, and that the discoverer of the strike was granted double, which meant three between them. They rushed back to their muddy creek the next morning and staked out another thousand feet, marking it *One Below* and

Two Below. Injun put Goat down as the discoverer and himself as the second man, but that was just a formality.

In Fortymile they borrowed a mule to haul their outfit and a stack of raw lumber to their claim for building a tiny cabin. They left two stumps in the middle of the floor to sit on, and built bunks against the walls. The windows were deer hide (that was a tip another old-timer had given them); Injun was surprised how well they let in the autumn light. With a sheet-iron stove they were all set, and Injun soon had some flapjacks on.

At first he couldn't get the knack of sleeping on his skinny bunk instead of back-to-back in the tent, but at least it was warmer. The walls smelled of sawdust, and pressed close, it was like living in a two-man coffin. Lucky we've got no third mate, he said in the dark.

Reckon so, Goat replied.

After a couple of days the cabin was fetid with smoke and feet. Injun pasted woodcuts from yellowed newspapers over the cracks: *Jumbo the Elephant,* and *Ladies Admiring Niagara Falls,* and *A View of Kew.* He found one called *The Forests of Scandinavia* to make his partner feel at home, not that Goat gave any sign of noticing. On the back, there was an article about some rich German with a bee in his bonnet about bringing all the creatures mentioned in Shakespeare to America; he'd released forty pairs of starlings in the middle of New York City. Bet they all got eat by nightfall, said Injun with a laugh, but Goat said naw, immigrants always take over, they've got fire in the belly.

In September, the leaves burned red and fell, and all the

Yukon's little veins froze up. Goat and Injun were so green, they'd never thought to wonder how to mine in the sub-Arctic winter. Sure, you have to burn your way down, said the Irish fellows on the next creek over. So every night the two partners lit a wood fire in their dig, and every morning they scraped past the ashes into the hot thawed earth. The greasy black shaft they hollowed out this way was barely wide enough to let one man crouch. The other would winch the bucket of muck up with a windlass, and pile it in a dump. It was a fortnight before they hit the pay streak—a dried-up creek channel—and started tunneling sideways along it. Already their pay-dirt dump was as high as Injun's head. But the killing thing about northern mining, of course, was you never knew what you'd got till the spring melt.

Sometimes they got so tired of the crawling and scrabbling in the smoky dark, they splashed their faces with water and trudged into Fortymile. There was a snowed-in vaudeville troupe that gave the same turns every night till the crowd howled like malamutes. There were ten saloons, and the code was that any man who came in with a poke of gold dust to throw down on the bar bought hot hootchinoo for everyone in hearing, or real whiskey if a boat had come in. Fortymile men all seemed to have got strange nicknames like Squaw Cameron or Cannibal Ike. (Goat and Injun were too used to their own monikers to remember they'd ever been called anything else.) The stories told in the saloons were of gold men; lucky ones, unlucky ones. A drunken sucker who got tricked into buying what seemed like a worthless stake, but it turned out a bonanza in the end. A Forty-Niner who washed out thirty thousand dollars but got so fixed on the prospect of being robbed that he slit his own throat before anyone else could.

The weather tightened like a fist. By October the two mates had stopped shaving, since a beard was some protection even if it did form icicles around the mouth. Injun's droopy Indian-style mustache flowed right into his side whiskers, he was like some old walrus, and Goat's goatee had spread into a yellow thornbush. When it got to fifty below, they gave up digging, lay in their bunks half the day in the smoky cabin. One of them might lurch out with scarves wrapped round his face to hack a deep hole in the river for water, or hobble into Fortymile—they were both plagued with blisters and boils on their feet—to get another handful of beans on credit. Long nights they curled like grubs in their foul sleeping bags, listing fresh things they'd a fancy for: apricots, cherries, tomatoes. They sang "My Darling Clementine" and "Break the News to Mother" and other old tunes they could only half remember. Injun hummed hymns from his childhood and Goat dredged up some sad Swedish songs. What's sad about them? Injun wanted to know, but Goat couldn't translate the words, he said, they're just sad.

The code was, show your grit, but help other gold men out, because otherwise who'd last a winter? A fellow was entitled to walk into your cabin while you were out, eat his fill, have a kip, and go on his way, as long as he left a supply of fresh kindling in case you came in frozen. Once Injun arrived home to find Goat talking Swedish with some block-faced stranger over the last of yesterday's bread. He didn't like the fellow's manner and was glad he was gone in the morning.

That winter the mates made all the mistakes of all young men in too much of a hurry to ask. They got stomachache when they didn't bother cooking their beans long enough, and toe rot from sleeping in wet boots. The one thing they knew never to do was let the fire die out, because of that popular story about the two partners discovered in an isolated cabin, stiff as rocks beside an icy stew kettle with nothing but a pair of partly cooked moccasins in it.

In the night Goat and Injun kept talking, speech slurred from numb lips, just so they'd know they hadn't died. Your Yukon is a perverse kind of river, remarked Injun, did you know it rises fifteen miles from the Pacific and then meanders around for two thousand more before it falls back down into the Pacific?

Goat grunted as if to say he neither knew nor cared. After a minute he said this cussed place, why did Uncle Sam ever buy it off the Ruskies?

He didn't, Injun corrected him, that's Alaska, we're in the Queen's territory now.

Goat muttered something about what he'd like to do to the Queen.

Soap out that filthy mouth, said Injun, coughing with laughter, don't you know she's about a hundred years old?

Came a long blizzard when water iced on the walls two feet from the fire. Let me in before I freeze, said Goat, stumbling two steps from his bunk to Injun's. Lying like spoons they shuddered up some warmth. Injun woke from a doze to find his hand on Goat's britches and he couldn't rightly have said whether it was him who'd put it there. His left hand was so numb it hardly knew what his right hand was doing and kept on doing. Then Goat thrashed round to face him and their breath was a hot Chinook wind.

What time is it, Injun wondered, what seemed like days later, and Goat said, what does it matter? They stirred and slept, touched and rolled and slept, couldn't get out of the bunk except once in a while to throw a log on the fire. You do it. No, you! Numbskull Swede, lazy half-breed, they cursed each other with a curious fondness, tried to shove each other onto the floor, grabbed each other again. The wind made a fearful whining.

There was something wrong with their legs, they were bruised blue and red. Injun's joints ached and his mouth tasted metallic, like blood. Is my breath bad? he asked. Goat, and his mate said, sure, but I don't care. Goat's face was strangely puffy. We're a couple of beauties, he wheezed, laying his yellow beard against Injun's bared chest.

Injun woke up later, unnerved by the silence. The blizzard had to be over. He was starving and sore. Slowly he heaved Goat against the wall, tucking the sleeping bag round him, and got to his feet. He took a sip of water from the cup on the stove. His face in the tin plate was weirdly mottled. What had they done to themselves? It occurred to him that they were dying and his heart lifted oddly.

It took Injun the best part of the day to stagger into Fortymile. My partner and I, we're dying of gangrene, he told McQuesten, taking down his trousers in the back of the store. The owner snorted and said, don't you fool boys know about scurvy? He sent Injun off with a bottle of lime juice, so sour it made him retch.

On the journey back, the sun came up over the ice, and Injun had forgotten his wooden mask with the slit in it. By the time he made it home he was so snowblind he was surprised he hadn't stumbled into some abandoned shaft and snapped his legs. His eyes were full of scalding sand, the good one as bad as the bad; the whole world was scarlet with fire, and the more he rubbed, the worse it hurt. Goat laughed but spooned stew into Injun's mouth like a mother.

Any way you looked at it, these were awful days. They'd come all this way to work like half-starved galley slaves. Even after the lime juice fixed their scurvy, they had a damaged look about them. Some mornings Injun stumbled through the dusk, past the smog rising from their shaft, to peer at the brooding outline of their dump. How much was black dirt, how much gold? A tree made a sound like a pistol shot and Injun jumped before remembering it was only the sap freezing. He could make out the purgatorial glow of other shafts on the next creek over, but the snow muffled all sounds. The world was empty but for small creeping things in their holes. He felt entirely temporary, and it occurred to him that the mine he and Goat were so painstakingly thawing and grubbing out this winter would, in years to come, close over again like a scar. Fortymile would fall to dust and wolves would bed down in these shacks, the ice would seal over the trail.

But Injun always finished what he set his hand to and Goat

was the same way. Also there was no way to Outside till spring unless they were insane enough to trek a thousand miles over the mountains. Also things had been different between them since the blizzard, they kept their kit on one bunk and slept on the other, or lay shoving and laughing and groaning in the dark. It was like a pact they didn't need to discuss.

Come May, at last, the cabin was green with mildew and the two partners coughed so wetly in the mornings it sounded like branches ripping off a tree. The crecks began to shrug off their ice; Injun and Goat's shaft seeped up to head height and they had to abandon it. It was time to build a long sluice box and divert some of the creek through it; time to see what they'd earned for their winter's punishment. They soon got a rhythm going: dump in a shovel of paydirt, let the water sweep the dross away, leaving the gold caught in the cross-riffles and matting at the bottom. Every three days they did a cleanup, lifting out the sluice box and panning the residue.

After the first week it was becoming clear to Injun that they were losers.

Goat would hear nothing of it. The good stuff's lower down the heap, he insisted.

Injun rolled his eyes. The black dirt was speckled with gold, all right, but so was every sandbank in this part of the world. Their poke was mounting up slowly, miserably, but other men lurched into Fortymile screaming like ravens, their pockets bursting with Midas dust. Gold men went on sprees from saloon to saloon, the crowd bearing them along like champions, smashing furniture. The Irishmen on the next creek over boasted of washing out twenty, twenty-five cents a pan. Fortunes were made and drunk all that summer, while Goat and Injun bent and sweated their strength away.

One day Goat said he'd had it.

What do you mean, you've had it?

I've had it up to here with gold mining.

Injun told him he just needed a whiskey. They walked into Fortymile, barely exchanging ten words along the way. Frost was tinting the mountains yellow already, the summer was on the turn. Injun picked up a page of newspaper in the street, it said the tenth of August. He blinked at it. Lookit, Goat, he said, I forgot my birthday. Yours too. Reckon we're twenty-three now.

Goat cleared his throat and spat before turning into the nearest saloon.

Injun went on to the store and handed over his meager poke, but McQuesten snorted as he weighed it in his hand, and tossed it back to him. He agreed to extend their credit a month or two longer, in case the boys' luck was around the corner. Injun's mouth felt gummed up with shame. If you fancy a change, McQuesten remarked, I could use someone in the back of the store.

Injun stared at him.

I had a boy, but he's gone rushing off downriver at the first word of some discovery.

Thank you, said Injun, remembering his manners like some old relic of life before the Yukon. Thank you kindly, but my partner—

McQuesten nodded like he understood.

On the way back down the street, Injun thought of how it might be. If Goat had had enough of mining, if Injun took a job in town—then they wouldn't be mates like they'd been. There'd be no reason for their cabin, their games, their joint life. He made up his mind: he'd talk Goat into heading back out to their claim and laying into that dirt-heap again. Maybe there really was more gold at the bottom. Maybe they should give it another year.

The saloon was buzzing. Goat shoved a glass of whiskey to his mate's lips. There's been a prime strike on Rabbit Creek!

Where's Rabbit Creek?

Off the Klondike.

The Klondike was the next big tributary of the Yukon east of Fortymile. That must be where McQuesten's last boy had gone. Injun felt oddly tired.

A fellow came in here with a shotgun cartridge full, Goat gabbled, poured it on the scale, old-timers never seen anything like it for color and grain. I tell you, boy, it's going to be a stampede! Let's go before every inch is staked. Half this crowd's slipped away already, he said, draining his glass.

Injun snorted, but already he was imagining their hands yellow-green with gold dust, their raw new shack on the bank of the Klondike.

Goat was looking past him, waving at someone in the crowd. Oh, hey, I met up with Gundsson again, he's on for going thirds.

Injun turned, narrowed his eyes at the big-jawed man

walking over. He recognized the Swede who'd turned up at the cabin that time. His throat tightened up. What do we need another mate for?

Goat laughed. Split the work and help tote the treasure sacks, that's what.

Could Goat really be that dumb and blind? Had he no notion of what they'd be losing? I don't like him, said Injun.

You ain't even talked to him yet. Come on, don't frown, sounds like there's gold enough for everyone up on the Klondike!

The Swede was beside them, grinning with yellow teeth. Injun thought of him sleeping in their cabin, like some huge stinking bear, and wanted to punch him. Instead he folded his arms. Gold men are so fickle, he remarked, soon as they hear of any half-discovery, they'll desert their old dig.

Goat tugged his mate's shoulder hard enough to pop it out. Look, you cussed half-breed, he said, can't your one eye spot the chance of your life?

Injun shrugged.

I tell you, I've talked to a man who saw the nuggets on the scale. He says he heard the first shovelful from Rabbit Creek yielded eight hundred dollars!

This place has more liars than hell, said Injun.

What's the matter with you? Goat was red in the face. The river's choked already. Fortymile will be a dead camp by the morning. Come on, Gundsson can get us on a boat poling upstream tonight.

Injun refused to look at the Swede. I'm taking a job, he said, his voice thick with gravel. In McQuesten's store.

Goat's eyes were huge and pale.

Folk'll always need supplies, he added. Even if some of these fools find a few ounces on the Klondike, they'll be back here to record their stakes, won't they?

Mate, said Goat—putting his face close enough to Injun's to heat him with his spiritous breath, close enough to kiss him—our fortune's up there. He was pointing east.

I doubt that, said Injun, hoarse.

But I'm telling you—

Finders ain't keepers anyhow. Men who strike lucky, they never manage to keep it, do they? Just drink or gamble or lose it all one way or another.

Goat straightened up, still half smiling. Well damn your lily liver.

Best of luck to you and your countryman, so, said Injun, going to drain his glass, but it was dry already. He told Goat to take what he liked from the cabin before he went. He nodded to both Swedes and managed to get outside in the warm street before his face fell in on itself.

And with the certainty of a man who was still young, Injun said never, he said never, never again.

Snowblind

Klondike (1958), Pierre Berton's classic history of the last—and most frantic—international gold rush, inspired this story of two fictional partners in Fortymile as the news of the Klondike discovery hit in August 1896.

WICKENBURG, ARIZONA
1873

THE LONG WAY HOME

One hot afternoon, a man walks into a bar. Well, not strictly speaking a man, but the stained buckskins, the fringed and beaded jacket, the stink of cigarillo, the small face leathered and squinting under the wide hat—what would you call it?

"How's business, Mollie?" asks the barkeep, filling a glass.

She takes her whiskey in two long, wet gulps. "Wouldn't know. I've been in the hills for a fortnight."

A red-haired man laughs, and remarks, to no one in particular, "It's a female."

He must be new to Wickenburg. "Prospecting?" suggests the barkeep.

She purses her dry lips.

He chuckles.

She considers the faces that line the bar. "Which one of these saddle bums goes by Jensen?"

"Here's what's left of him." With one finger the barkeep indicates the man sleeping half off his stool: a puddle of greasy hair, a hat tipped sideways on the wet wood.

Mollie blows out her breath and pours herself another.

"What d'you want with my aul pal Jensen?" demands the redhead.

"Four days since he rode into town for supplies," she tells him, "left his wife in an empty camp. I'm taking him back."

"Can't a man spend his poke in peace?"

She walks over to Jensen. Her hands slide into his pockets, down his legs. He grunts.

"C'mere, wee lassie," croons the Irishman, "don't be wasting that on a sleeping man." He shuffles up close behind her. "And what have *you* got in your pocket?"

"A Peacemaker," says Mollie under her breath before he can touch her. Finding Jensen's little bag, she straightens up, and drops it on the bar.

The barkeep's scowl deepens as he sets it on the scales. "That won't half cover his tab."

"Guess I'll have to take up a collection, then." She lifts the drunk's hat and holds it out in front of the Irishman.

"Here's all I've got for you," he says, and spits in it.

He must not have believed her about the pistol, so she moves her coat and shows him a glimpse of its thick barrel. "In that case, should I shoot your jewels off right this minute, or would you rather help me with your *aul pal* here?"

The Irishman steps back, paler under his burn. "What kind of help?"

"Check his cayuse's well watered."

While he's outside, she goes round with the hat, laying on the charm. "Come on, men, a bit of actual? I've spent all mine on provisions for the Jensens," she assures them. "Let's clear the bum's tab and I undertake to get him home by to-morrow, what do you say?"

There's protest and eye rolling and jokes about lady boun-tifuls, but they pay up. The Irishman comes back in and produces half a dollar.

"Stay for a round of faro, why don't you, Mollie," sug-gests a farmer.

She grins, hovering by the table, then shakes her head.

She takes the unconscious Jensen by his collar and yanks him onto the floor. He's coming to by the time she's dragged him to the door—twisting against the light of the lamps, starting to babble—so she gets the Irishman to grab his feet. They haul him like wet washing; another two men help heave him into the saddle of his hungry-looking horse.

She rides up alongside and plants the groggy man's hat on his head. "Name's Mollie Monroe," she tells him. "Going to ride behind me without a ruckus?"

Apparently not. She ducks away from his fist; her pony shies. "Better lash his hands to the pommel," she tells the Irishman. "And pass me his rifle." She ties it behind her saddle, on top of the sacks of beans and meal. She coils his horse's rope around her wrist and murmurs "Gitty up" to her own.

All through town Jensen curses. Damns the dust, the lin-gering heat of the August day, but most of all damns this half-size freak in britches, this vigilante morphodite who's got him roped like some felon when last he heard this was the free state of Arizona. He pukes and spatters his leg.

It's going to be a long ride. Mollie passes the bright windows of her own saloon. Looks like George's got his hands full this Saturday night. Shame she hasn't time to stop in for a quick one, but it would only start a quarrel, likely.

The lush banks of the Hassayampa drop out of sight behind them. Scattered saguaros stick up like fists against the orange evening as she heads toward Black Mountain, a road some call cursed, since a stagecoach full of passengers got themselves massacred a few winters past.

Behind her, Jensen's retching drily. She walks her pony back, reins in at arm's length, and hands over the water bag.

His eyes are red-rimmed as he drinks. "Cut me loose," he says, half-baring his teeth, "or I swear, I won't leave enough of you to snore."

Mollie keeps her grin on. "Do I look scairt?"

"Crazy as popcorn on a stove, that's what you look."

"Don't push me, Jensen. I'd rather deliver you in one piece." She clicks her tongue to start her pony moving again.

"Deliver me to who?" The question comes hoarsely.

She's sorely tempted not to answer; to let Jensen spend a few minutes—even hours—recollecting his enemies. Instead, she says over her shoulder, "Your wife."

"How the blazes do you know my wife?" he demands, bends to puke again but there's nothing in it.

She reins in, lets him catch up. "I was riding by a mine shaft this morning, your boy was down it, his mama was screaming for him to climb out. Fine pair you've got, and another one coming any day, looks like; she can hardly get around. They'll be a big help with the prospecting in another few years, that's if any of them last that long."

"What do you know about prospecting?" he asks with venom.

She rides on. "Oh, me and George Monroe have staked claims all over these hills. Once I sold a bonanza for twenty-five hundred dollar, blew it all in a week!"

"I've heard of Monroe," concedes Jensen. "But I never heard tell he was married."

She sets her teeth. Hasn't she a right to the name after all these years? "Mrs. Jensen seems a nice piece of Mexican calico," she throws over her shoulder.

"Is she paying you?" Jensen wants to know.

"Ha! With what?"

He doesn't speak again.

She turns off the road onto a dry wash, heading south into the foothills. The night is crisp now, stars pricking a black sky. She glances back, and Jensen's dropped his head on his bound hands. She's suddenly beat.

The man's no help to her; slumps against the furrowed trunk of a cottonwood as she stokes the fire with what dried dung she can find. "Never thought we'd run out of bison shit," she remarks, "but now they've got those excursion trains, shoot from the windows, you ever hear of such a thing?"

No response. Not even when Mollie serves up her famous stew. (She's cooked for fifty at a time, and never heard any complaints.) She undoes the knot that holds Jensen's wrists together, but keeps her pistol handy. The plate shudders in his hands. A cool northern breeze angles off the mountains, which are only starless patches on the sky. Jensen suddenly lurches to his feet and goes behind a saguaro. Got the trots, Mollie reckons; that's the end of many a spree. When he comes back, he crouches and breaks off a corner from the nearest outcropping, peers at it; one of those prospector's habits.

Mollie binds his hands again, adds a rope around his ankle, and throws him a blanket before she settles down on her bedroll with the horses' ropes under her. The pistol digs into her hip as she drops into sleep.

In the gray dawn, the end of Jensen's rope lies blackened in the ashes. "Well, that's just daisy," Mollie mutters, through a yawn. She's mildly impressed, though he didn't manage to sneak his horse away from her, or his rifle.

She follows his tracks back toward Wickenburg, catching up with him in a quarter of an hour. From a distance, he looks like some mad preacher, stalking along with joined hands.

Mollie reins in beside him. He's got a healthier color than yesterday, at least. He stops, panting slightly.

"Care to ride?" she asks, indicating his horse.

"Care to go fuck yourself?"

Men often think to scandalize her, which is funny. As if, under the buckskins, there's still some fragile lady, trembling at each dirty word.

"You're a cross-grained son of a bitch, aren't you?" she remarks, putting Jensen on a long rope. "Don't seem to care how hungry that family of yours gets. Course, all alone in that godforsaken camp since Tuesday, they could have been scalped by now."

His eyes glitter. "No Apaches left south of Prescott."

"Yeah, sure, except for the odd renegade in the hills. Or of course any white desperadoes who might see Mrs. J's fire, they'd be sure to treat her like gentlemen."

She lets him mull that over. Clicks to her horse, moving off at a walk so Jensen has to stumble along behind. If this takes three days, he'll just have to tell his wife they went the long way.

He jerks, drags his feet, curses.

At one point he trips and can't seem to get to his feet again. For a minute she lets the horse pull him along in the dust—but he won't be much good to Mrs. J. all shredded, so Mollie calls a halt. "Get on your cayuse, or we're gonna be baking out here all week."

It could go either way.

But Jensen climbs up into the saddle, and on they ride. Southwest, keeping Twin Peaks on the right and Vulture Peak on the left.

"Old Vulture's given up over thirty million dollars in gold," Mollie remarks.

"Not to me, she hasn't."

Mollie's watching the horizon for dust storms. Below them the Sonoran desert stretches away, already shimmering. Jensen's botched escape has cost them an hour, so they have to ride hard in the heat of the afternoon to have any chance of reaching the camp by nightfall. A little scrub oak and piñon juniper for shade, but every crick they pass is dry; Mollie doles out the water bag sparingly. It's too hot to talk; she rubs her gritty eyes and urges her pony on.

"Come on," says Jensen suddenly, "has my wife promised you something she's got stashed away, from her papa?"

"She's got nothing," says Mollie, "except another little Jensen about to carve its way out of her."

He stares. "You some class of do-gooder?"

"It was a slack week."

The fact is, she does make a habit of this kind of thing. Hears of a man sick in camp, rides out with medicine and rabbit soup. Adventure's scarce since the Indian Wars ended.

As darkness moves over the hills, she decides they must be another hour from Jensen's camp, and it isn't worth breaking her pony's leg.

She likes to sing while she's cooking. Jensen pulls a face: "Somebody forgot to grease the wagon."

When she serves up the doings, he holds out his bound hands. "Let me hold my fork."

"Not till you're home."

"For blazes' sake, I'm not some lost steer."

"A steer would have more sense."

It may be foolish, but she undoes the knot anyway. Jensen flexes his hands, shakes them, rubs them where they're chafed.

Mollie doles out a small measure of whiskey. "Here's how," she says, for a toast.

They swap tales of veins and lodes they have known, as sailors talk of their ships.

"I wear the clothes that fit the work," says Mollie, "but they get me arrested every now and then."

"Arrested?"

"Impersonating a man, so-called."

"Huh." He shakes his head. "I wouldn't mistake you."

They have a cigarillo each. Jensen's followed gold all over the map: Nevada, Boise, Salt Lake City. Got bit by a rattlesnake one time. "Never gone looking for a bullet," he mentions, "but I've always thought that if one happened my way, it wouldn't make no odds."

She leans to top up his mug.

"I still reckon you're getting something out of this business," he says suddenly.

For a minute she thinks "this business" means life. Then she gets it, almost laughs, lets out a long sigh instead. "Well, I can't fool you, Jensen. Your wife did promise me something I've always had a hankering for."

"I knew it!"

"Something you'll hardly miss."

"What is it?"

Very quiet. "A child."

The fire crackles. Jensen stares at her over his smeared plate. His mouth moves before he speaks. The word comes out hoarse. "Which one?"

She would have liked to keep it up a bit longer but she can't stop the sound, it bubbles up, it whoops out into the starry night.

Jensen's plate is overturned, he's jumped the fire, he's on top of her. "You dyed-in-the-wool bastard."

Mollie's helpless with glee. "*Which one?*" is all she can squeak: "*Which one?*"

His hands are on her throat. She can't reach her Peacemaker, this could very well be the end of Mollie Monroe, the all too likely squalid end for a woman of her peculiarities, left throttled by a dying campfire, but still she can't stop laughing.

Jensen's teeth are very close to hers. They've stopped moving. "You're as ugly as a burnt boot," he informs her.

"Mm-hm."

"Face like a dime's worth of dog meat."

Mollie lets out a small groan. "Oh, fish or cut bait, won't you?"

She pulls down her own pants before he can. He goes at her hammer and tongs. Like a wolf, like she likes it. His flesh a stone pounding her to dust. Sand in her face and her own gun bruising her thigh.

They sleep back-to-back for heat.

Up before the sun. The mountains stand gray and sawtoothed. Mollie doesn't make coffee. They pack in silence, without looking at each other, like two old prospectors. Jensen takes back his rifle.

When the little camp comes into sight around a bend, she says, "Hey! Finally shed of you. You going to do the clean thing now, make the bettermost of it?"

He speaks between his teeth. "Next time you set yourself up for judge and jury—"

"Christ almighty," she says, "who am I to judge? I've woken up in my own puke on a poker table."

He's looking right past her at the tent with the fire smoking outside it.

Mollie reins in her horse. Turns to undo the packs of supplies.

"Will you have some breakfast?" His eyes are scanning the rocks for his children.

"I won't."

He shakes her hand.

"Give my respects to Monroe."

"And mine to Mrs. Jensen." Mollie clicks her tongue to her horse, turns back toward Wickenburg.

The Long Way Home

Mollie (born Mary) Sanger, born somewhere in New England in 1836 or perhaps 1846, arrived in Arizona as the wife of a lieutenant in the mid-1860s but soon paired up with George Monroe and worked as a prospector, cowboy, cook, and saloonkeeper. This story, about a (possibly apocryphal) incident from the early 1870s in which she dragged a prospector back to his family, draws on two articles, "Mollie Monroe: Memorable, 'Crazy' Character of Early Prescott," in *Sharlot Hall Museum: Days Past* (November 2, 1997), and Nell Simcox's "The Story of Mollie Monroe: Girl Cowboy," in *Real West Magazine* (April 1983).

A few years later, Mollie moved from Wickenburg back to Prescott (apparently without George Monroe). In 1877 she was the first woman in Arizona committed for insanity, which probably translates as cross-dressing, promiscuity, and alcoholism. In 1895 Mollie Monroe escaped from Phoenix Asylum and roamed the desert for four days, surviving on one bottle of water and a few crackers, before being recaptured by Indian trackers. After a quarter century of confinement, she died in 1902.

CHICAGO
1876

THE BODY SWAP

A rainy October night at the Hub on Chicago's West Madison Street. Mullen, the jewel-eyed little barman, smoothes his thick mustache and tops up Morrissey's glass. He leans one elbow on the sodden plank bar, considers the young man, then jerks his head toward the back. Morrissey has been fraternizing at the Hub for some weeks, telling stories of his time in Wisconsin State, but this is the first time Mullen's invited him into his office.

It's as plain as the front but smells better. There's a sad-eyed character there already, sandy beard half-covering impassive features. "Hughes," says Mullen, with only a trace of a brogue, "this is Morrissey that I was telling you of."

The older man sticks out his hand.

Morrissey shakes it, and accepts a broken-backed chair. "So what's on?"

Hughes looks sideways at the Hub's proprietor. "He knows nothing?"

"I could hardly go into it at the bar." Mullen sits down and pours three shots.

"I'm hoping you gentleman have a mind to bring me in on some business," Morrissey volunteers.

"What kind of business?" asks the older man.

"Oh, come on, Mr. Hughes. The coney trade, the bogus; shoving the queer."

"Knowing the lingo doesn't mean knowing the business," observes Hughes.

"I never claimed to. The proverbial blank slate, that's me. You need a shover, is that it? I could pass bad bills with a straight face."

Hughes releases a sigh like air from a tire. "The business is all done in."

Morrissey looks taken aback. "You say?"

"Time was, there was more queer than good floating round Illinois," Hughes laments. "With all those newfangled notes and greenbacks the Government printed during the War between the States, who could tell bogus at a glance? But since they formed this Secret Service to crack down on us, trade's turned tight as blazes."

"It used to be you could bribe them to turn a blind eye," Mullen contributes, "but these days..."

"And now they've banged up our Michelangelo."

The young man blinks at Hughes. "Your—"

"Ever hear of Ben Boyd?"

"Can't say as how I have," admits Morrissey.

Another sigh. "In any other field of art or industry, the man's name would be on every child's tongue. But Boyd works on the quiet, like some angel."

"A friend of yours?"

"Ben Boyd is only the greatest living engraver of queer. Living *or* dead," Hughes insists.

"We've never met him in the flesh," Mullen adds.

"But by his works we know him."

"You'd swear you're looking at a genuine silk-thread Federal banknote," Mullen tells Morrissey. "Big Jim wholesales them all over the Mid West. You know Big Jim?"

"Well, sure; I know of him." Big Jim Kinealy is the Hub's silent partner, the mover behind all business conducted in this room.

Hughes takes up the story. "But nothing's moving these days. Since January, Ben Boyd's been in Joliet State, doing his first year of ten."

The young man winces. "So your best supply's been cut off."

"The only coney worth a bean," Hughes corrects him. "What's out there wouldn't fool a nun."

Silence; they all drink their rum.

"I'm truly sorry for your troubles, gentlemen," says Morrissey, "but where do I come in?"

"Not just for our own sakes but for the sake of the whole profession," says Hughes, "Boyd must be sprung."

Morrissey lets out a small laugh. "Horse stealing or a touch of safe-cracking, and I'm your man, but—"

Mullen waves one finger to shut him up. "Big Jim has a plan. We're going to spring Boyd, make our fortunes, and go down in history, all at the self-same time."

"Is that a fact," murmurs Morrissey.

"Are you in?" Hughes wants to know.

"Oh, come on, now, it's only white to tell a fellow what he'll be getting into first."

The barman curls his lip. "You think I'm going to lay out our design and have you walk away and blab it all over Chicago?"

Morrissey spits to show what he thinks of blabbers. "I'd be considerable of an idiot to say I'm in till I hear the details, but my lips are sewn."

"Go on," Mullen tells Hughes, "he's all right."

Hughes shifts his chair a little closer to the table and tops up his glass. "What would you say is the perfect swag?"

Morrissey stares at him.

"Take a guess. The ideal booty."

"Something worth a lot...that's easy to take, and fits in your pocket," hazards Morrissey.

Hughes shakes his sandy head. "If it's worth a lot, and if you're tumbled, you'll do a lot of time."

"But if it's not worth much...why trouble?"

Mullen sniggers.

Hughes delivers the answer like Scripture: "The perfect swag is something worth nothing, that people will pay high for."

Morrissey looks between the two men. "Is this some class of a confidence trick? Like, the mark thinks there's a diamond in the empty box?"

"No," says Hughes, stroking his beard, "no deception's involved."

"Think it through," Mullen teases.

"I am doing." Sulky now. "Something worth nothing... what, nothing at all, like water or dirt?"

Hughes raps the table. "You're getting warm."

"Which?"

"Dirt."

"You've a mind to steal dirt?" Morrissey asks.

"A special kind of dirt."

"A body of dirt, you might say." Mullen grins as he slicks back his hair. "Dust to dust!"

"Oh, I get it." Morrissey lets out a whistle, then lowers his voice. "You're talking to a veteran body snatcher, as it just so happens. Back in Wisconsin I dug up a dozen or so, sold them to the medical school."

"We heard that story," Mullen tells him. "That's why we figured you might want to make a stake with us."

"But selling to doctors is not our game," says Hughes with disdain. "You ever hear of the Trojan War?"

"I reckon." Morrissey's voice is uncertain.

"This one fellow did for another fellow, and then he went one better on it, because he ransomed the corpse back to the fellow's pa for its weight in gold."

"Naw!"

"And the best thing is, the State of Illinois's got no law against the stealing of a cadaver," Mullen puts in. "It's no-body's property once it's stopped breathing. The most we could be pulled for is the price of the coffin, and that can't mean more than a year in jail."

"But whose coffin?" asks Morrissey. "Just what body are we talking about?"

"No need for names," says Hughes before Mullen's got the first syllable out. "Come on out to the bar for a minute."

"You jokers are just pulling my leg," says Morrissey,

pushing back his chair. "What, is he one of the regulars?"

Mullen shakes his head. "He took a bullet eleven years back."

The Hub is filling up when they emerge: six men at the billiards table, another dozen hanging on the bar, getting impatient. Hughes lets his eyes flicker to the wall above the bottles. Morrissey follows his glance to the plaster bust of Abraham Lincoln.

November 6, the night before the election, the three men press through a Democratic torchlight parade to the station. They get on the nine o'clock train to Springfield, taking over an empty carriage. Mullen drops a clanking tool bag.

"Mind my foot," objects Morrissey, pulling it out from under.

"Put it up in the compartment, Mullen," says Hughes. "Are you drunk?"

"Just a little jollified, in honor of our venture," Mullen tells him. "Accepted three Democrat shots and four Republican ones."

"You've got to play fair," agrees Morrissey, grinning.

"It's a sad fact about our line of business that it requires a nomadic sort of existence, since laying low prevents registering to vote," remarks Hughes, making himself comfortable by the window. "If it were otherwise I believe I'd give my ticket to Governor Hayes, seeing as he's a war hero."

Mullen snorts. "Uncle Sammy Tilden's going to sweep in and clean house. High time we pulled our troops home and left the South to solve its own hell-fired problems."

Hughes's eyebrows soared. "The barman is a citizen of views," he told Morrissey. "Most of them claptrap."

"I reckon this election will be the closest thing that ever was, anyhow," contributes Morrissey.

"Five bucks, says Tilden," mutters Mullen.

Hughes bursts out laughing.

"What now?"

"Five bucks? What a small-timer you are, Mullen. By the time this job's done, as well as getting Boyd out, we'll each have bagged a sixth of two hundred thousand dollars!"

The figure seems to make the air in the carriage ripple.

"Yeah, but five's all I've got in my pocket just at present," says Mullen.

Morrissey's smooth forehead is wrinkling. "A sixth of it? There's four of us, counting Billy Brown..."

"Right, but Big Jim planned it with Nelson before ever we came in, so they've earned their cuts of the ransom."

"I suppose," says Morrissey. "Though we're the ones risking life and limb."

Mullen makes a chicken squawk and punches Morrissey in the arm. "We're risking nothing, boy. On Election Night, with all creation in the streets, who'll notice another wagon heading out of Springfield? It's a perfect time for a daredevil trip. A damn elegant time."

"You're drunk," Hughes observes again. "Bridget says if you turn up pie-eyed at the church, she's going to walk away."

"Who's Bridget?" Morrissey wants to know.

"My dear and only widowed sister," says Hughes.

"My fiancée," Mullen corrects him with a wide grin. "Hey, with my share, I'll be able to buy her such a mansion, she'll thank me on bended knee."

"You may be going to marry her," mutters Hughes, "but you don't know her." He turns to Morrissey. "You still huffed about your share?"

"Naw, that's all right."

"There's six men in this mob, so six is how it cuts. Nobody's out to swindle you. Thirty-three thousand, son— that'll take you the rest of your life to blow."

Morrissey nods, summons a grin.

The engine lets out a long, hoarse whistle, and they fall silent. "I saw his funeral train pull into Chicago," remarks Hughes.

"Whose?"

Hughes gives Morrissey an exasperated look. "Honest Abe's, of course, eleven years back. The *Lincoln Express,* hung with black drapery and evergreens. It zigzagged all the way from Washington, D.C., to Springfield, going no faster than a boy could run. You never saw such a procession: all along the tracks were crowds standing to pay their respects, day and night."

"Fancy that."

"I even joined the line at the courthouse, saw his face."

"How was he looking?" Mullen wants to know.

"Not his best. This was a full fortnight after the assassination," Hughes points out.

"But hadn't they—I mean—"

"Embalmed him? Of course they had: pickled like a cu-

cumber. They don't let the famous rot. But his face was greenish."

"How—how do you reckon he'll be now?" murmurs Mullen. "Just bones?"

"Naw, I'd say still pickled. A mummy, near as like."

"We haven't got to take him out of his casket, do we?" asks Morrissey.

Hughes shrugs. "I hope not. But it's lead inside cedar according to the custodian; sounds heavy."

"Hughes and I did the full tour, to scout the place out," Mullen explains.

"If it proves too much for us three and Billy Brown, we might have to pull him out and bag him." Hughes shows them a burlap sack.

The other two stare at it. "I hope it's long enough," says Mullen. "Wasn't he a giant of a man?"

"Six foot four inches in his socks," says Morrissey.

"Six six, I heard."

"We'll double him over, then," Hughes snaps.

Mullen sniffs. "We'd better take care of him, if he's worth so much, that's all I'm saying. They mightn't like to pay full price if he's in pieces."

The men from Chicago get in at 6 a.m. A cloudy, cold Election Day. Springfield is chaos crossed with carnival. Jollification booths, party ribbons, posters warning of forged voting ballots, bets taken everywhere you look, muscular characters grabbing voters outside the polling booths to whisper in their ears...

Mullen, Hughes, and Morrissey split up to be unobtrusive,

leaving the bag of tools with a bartender of Mullen's acquaintance. They kill the hours somehow; Hughes gets a shoe mended. In the afternoon there's a fight, and a negro voter gets his throat cut. As the day wears on, crowds swarm round the telegraph and newspaper offices, waiting for returns. Sam Tilden is thought to have it. Even this town—home to the Great Emancipator, the first Republican president—is said to have swung Democrat.

In their room at the St. Charles Hotel, Hughes squints at a map. "You know, I reckon it's too far to go all the way to the Indiana Sand Hills in this cold snap, we might get stopped."

Mullen's arms are folded. "But Big Jim said—"

"I don't know what he was thinking. You can't tell me there's nowhere to hide a body in the whole State of Illinois."

Mullen unfolds a smaller map of Sangamon County. "See this bridge across the river, just a mile or two east of the cemetery? We could dump the coffin on the upside, it'll sink to the bottom."

"What if it floats?" Morrissey asks.

"Lead-lined," Hughes reminds him.

The younger man flushes at his mistake. "All right, but what if the water's too shallow?"

"Then we'll dig a hole in the gravel bar under the shadow of the bridge." Hughes nods over the map. "The roads will be frozen hard, our horse tracks won't show. Where's your friend Brown going to get this rig?"

"He said he'd nab one easy, from some drunken farmer."

"Why can't he hire one?"

"He doesn't have the cash. Don't worry, he'll find us a good team."

"Oh, and I had a notion," says Mullen, producing a copy of that day's *Catholic Union and Times*. He rips off the front page, then tears that along a messy diagonal.

"What are you playing at?" asks the older man.

"Got this tip from an interview with a kidnapper," says Mullen. "We leave this half in the crypt, right? Then we hide the matching half somewhere safe—say, back in the Hub, inside that hollow bust of Lincoln. When Big Jim's negotiating, he can use it to prove we truly are the ones who did the deed."

Hughes nods, but soberly. "I don't mind allowing I'll be glad when this is all over, Boyd's back at his bogus, and I can return to honest work."

Morrissey sniggers. Hughes's head shoots up. "I only meant—I never heard it called that before," says the young man.

"You, sir, move in certain circles—horse thieves, burglars, and the like," says Hughes, "and I in others."

"What, ain't counterfeiters crooked?"

"Only technically. We do no harm to our fellow man."

"Oh, Jack, lay off your sham," Mullen puts in.

"Money's not real gold anymore," Hughes insists. "It's only a kind of paper that the government calls precious; it's a trick in itself. Well, I say Boyd's bad notes are just as good. Who am I robbing, tell me, if I buy a horse with a queer bill?"

"Well—"

"The man I pay can buy something else with it, if his luck holds. It all goes round."

"Tell that to the Secret Service," says Mullen with a broad grin. "He was arrested back in August, for shoving the coney," he tells Morrissey.

Hughes sighs. "After a dozen years of being careful, never going out with more than one note on me..."

"Skipped bail, too. That's how come he's let his beard grow into such an ugly bush so he can hide behind it."

"I was thinking," says Hughes, "when it comes to freeing Boyd and getting our reward, why couldn't we ask for the settlement of my own little case to be thrown in?"

Mullen shrugs. "You better take that up with Big Jim."

"I might well. I could eat like all wrath," says Hughes after a minute. "I'm going downstairs for a plate of oysters." The others follow him out of the room, but he turns. "We can't all go: three together could attract attention."

"On a night like this," scoffs Mullen, "you'd have to run bare-assed along Main Street to attract attention."

"No, he's right," says Morrissey, "I'll go eat elsewhere, check Brown's got us a wagon. See you back here at half past eight."

In the dark, the three of them walk along the streetcar tracks north of Springfield. Mullen is humming "I'll Take You Home Again, Kathleen." He's got an ax over one shoulder that he took from outside the tavern, on a whim. He pauses to adjust something in his armpit.

"You armed?" Morrissey asks him.

"Always. And it doesn't take a great deal of provocation to make me shoot."

"Mullen's an all-fired desperado, all right," says Hughes with a snort.

Morrissey hawks tobacco juice into a bush.

"So Brown will be at the cemetery by half past nine?" Hughes asks him.

"Yup, he's borrowed a three-spring wagon and a rattling good pair of bays. He'll tie them up in the woods, then come to the Monument and give the whistle."

Oak Ridge Cemetery is ahead. They jump the fence and move round through the trees. One small light flickers. "That's the custodian's lodge," murmurs Hughes.

At the top of the hill, on a small plateau, the Monument rears up in the patchy moonlight: an obelisk with statues of soldiers and horses swarming round its base. "Like something out of Old Egypt," Morrissey marvels. "It must be two hundred feet high."

"It's a solid-looking pile, all right," says Mullen.

"That bit that curves out the front is a little museum. The crypt is at the back," says Hughes.

Their approach is up a steep ravine, bare except for a single oak. Hughes pauses to take out a small bull's-eye lantern, rip the paper off, and light it. The wooden door has a simple lock; it doesn't take Morrissey long to pick it. Inside is another door, iron this time, with a steel bolt secured by a padlock. Mullen pulls out a jimmy and fits the sections together. He works on the padlock for some minutes. "Damn thing's too big for the staple."

"Try a steel saw," advises Hughes.

"That's just exactly what I was about to do." But the

metal resists his squealing blade. "Tarnation seize this good-for-nothing lock. I'm going to take the ax to it."

"That won't work." After a few more minutes Hughes taps Morrissey on the shoulder, making him jump. "You and I should check the front, just in case."

"In case of what?"

"In case there's a guard posted, or the custodian's got a notion to sit up with his President. Old men can't sleep."

"Hey," protests Mullen, "where're you fellows going with the light?"

"Can't you saw by starlight for a minute? You could hardly make a poorer fist of the job…"

Morrissey and Hughes go round to the front. The museum is quite dark. Hughes takes out a pistol. Morrissey slides open the shutter of the lantern, holds it against the outer bars and peers through the glass pane. "Nothing stirring."

When they get back, Mullen's saw has cut about a third of the way through the padlock. They lean against the wall and watch him. Suddenly the blade snaps. He hurls down the pieces. "This cock-sucking saw! I could cut steel better with a penknife."

"Don't blame the damn tools when it was you who chose them," says Hughes. "Here, try with a file."

Hughes hugs the bars to hold the padlock quite steady while Mullen goes to work with a three-cornered file.

"We can take turns if you get tuckered," offers Morrissey.

"I'm not tuckered," grunts Mullen. "Just you keep watch."

"I believe I'll take another tour around the Monument."

Morrissey walks silently round the side of the building. At the door of the museum he reaches through the bars and taps three times on the glass. A long pause, and then the door opens a crack. "Chief?" he whispers.

"I'll get him" comes the reply.

In a minute Chief Patrick Tyrrell puts his meaty-jawed head out, hisses, "What's the delay?"

"They're having trouble with the padlock."

A sharp sigh. "We'd better hang on till they've got the tomb open; otherwise it's only breaking and entering."

"How many of you are in there?" asks Morrissey, peering through the gap.

"Five, plus the custodian and a reporter. We've got these ghouls dead to rights," says Tyrrell, his voice gravelly with anticipation. "Tonight's operation is going to break the back of counterfeiting in the United States."

Morrissey is looking down: "How come you're in your socks, Chief?"

"We were afraid of making noise," Tyrrell hisses; "the marble echoes like the blazes. Go on back, before they come looking!"

Back outside the crypt, Morrissey finds Mullen working at the lock with a pair of pinchers, twisting it like taffy. He breaks off with a grunt and rubs his hands to warm them. "You ever tried this kind of business before?" he asks Hughes.

"What, lock breaking?"

"Grave robbing."

Hughes shakes his head.

"There's nothing to it, once we're in," Morrissey assures them. "We don't even have to dig, just get the lid off."

"If it wasn't for the need to spring Boyd out of jail," mutters Mullen, "I wouldn't quite like disturbing a man's rest."

"Oh, he's sleeping too deep to care," the older man tells him.

"Are you superstitious, Mullen?" jeers Morrissey.

A shrug. "No more than the next fellow. Old Abe himself did some table rapping. I heard it was spirits told him he had to free the slaves."

"I've got no bone to pick with the great man," Hughes tells him.

"No bone—I get it," says Mullen with a snigger.

"It's a bone for a bone, in this case," says Hughes, "a body for a body. There's a kind of justice to the exchange. The people of America will get their sainted Abe back in a week or two, as soon as we get Ben Boyd."

"Plus the two hundred thousand bucks," says Morrissey.

"Well, yeah. That's about how much the people of Illinois spent on this here eternal Monument," says Hughes, craning up at the obelisk, "so the contents must be worth at least as much."

"Plus, we'll get fame," adds Mullen, "and the respect of our fellow Americans!"

Hughes rolls his eyes at Morrissey.

With that, the lock finally cracks and falls. "All set," crows Mullen, "let her rip!"

Hughes hushes him. The door scrapes open. Morrissey hangs back, lets the other two go ahead.

"Morrissey!"

"I reckon I should keep watch...""

"Get in here and hold the light."

There in the middle of the crypt is the great marble sarcophagus, its end slab inscribed *LINCOLN*. Below, it says *With Malice toward None, with Charity for All.* The men approach slowly. "Well, here we are with our revered leader," murmurs Morrissey.

Mullen fingers the thin slab on the top, and the thinner one below it. "I don't reckon we're going to need the drill and gunpowder. I could smash this open easy," he pronounces. "Why, I could kick it open!"

"Exactly how much did you have to drink?" Hughes inquires.

"Just a little nerve tonic."

"This one here says Willie," says Morrissey, holding the lantern over the other tombs. "And here's Tad, and...little Eddie."

"Losing three sons out of four, that's no luck," comments Mullen, shaking his head.

"Can we get this done sometime before dawn?" demands Hughes.

"This one's blank," Morrissey points out.

"For Mrs. Lincoln," Mullen tells him.

"Didn't the other son put her in a nuthouse?"

"Naw, she skedaddled."

"You loafing bums," Hughes barks, "we've got a tomb to open. Shut pan and get to work."

Mullen heaves the stolen ax over his head.

"Hold up there," says Morrissey rapidly, grabbing the barman's arm.

"Watch yourself! I nearly had your hand off."

"The custodian's not so far off, he might hear you. And I reckon if we can prize the slab off in one piece, we can put it back afterward and then no one will know what we've taken, for a while anyhow."

"There's a plan," Hughes decides.

Sullen, Mullen shoves the edge of his ax under the marble, and it lifts with a creak. "Would you look at that, there's nothing but plaster holding it on!"

Between the three of them they drag the great slab to one side and rest it against the tomb set aside for Mrs. Lincoln. Now Mullen goes to work on the thinner slab with the ax blade. Morrissey uses a chisel. They manage to break the cement and pry the lid up at one corner, but it won't come off. "Let me smash it," says Mullen longingly.

"Wait a tick." Morrissey has found some copper dowels holding the sarcophagus together. "If we can just lift it clear of these pins..."

Grunting and growling, they manage it, and lay the marble across the tomb. "There she lies," says Mullen, peering in.

"She?"

"I meant the casket. The cedar."

Hughes is examining the end slab. "If we can pull this piece off, we can slide the thing out instead of having to lift it...Mullen, where's your jimmy?" He crowbars the copper ties, and lays the end slab on the floor. He and Mullen take hold of the coffin by its edges, and pull it about two feet out of the sarcophagus. Hughes straightens, wheezing a little. "I reckon it weighs about five hundred pounds."

"Let's take the lid off," suggests Mullen, eyes glittering.

"What for?" asks Hughes.

"Yeah," Morrissey laughs, "we can hardly have got the wrong fellow."

"Just to see. I bet he's all dark by now, like a bronze of himself. Do you reckon he still has his little chin-beard?"

"Half the men in America have his little chin-beard by now," Morrissey quips.

"Feel that," says Mullen, grabbing Morrissey's fist and putting it to his waistcoat. Morrissey pulls away. "My heart, it's going like a rattle."

"You skeery?" sneers Hughes.

"No I am not. Just excited. This is a historic moment. The real thing. Abe Lincoln in the flesh!"

Morrissey shakes his head. "It's only his mortal coil, that he shuffled off a long time back. The bird has flown."

"I don't know about that."

"Why, don't you believe you have a soul, you heathen?"

"I remain to be convinced. What am I, exactly, if I'm not this?" Mullen asks, grabbing a fistful of his arm. "Anyhow, I knew a pickpocket with an Indian skull for a paperweight, he never had any luck."

"I saw the Hottentot Venus in a freak show," Morrissey told him, "her corpse, I mean."

"How big was her quim?"

"Not as big as they said it would be."

Hughes has yanked out his watch. "Where's Billy Brown?"

"Yeah," says Mullen, "we should have heard his whistle by now."

"With all the ruckus you've been making, we wouldn't have heard the Last Trumpet."

"I'll go find him, I bet he's waiting in the trees," Morrissey volunteers, handing Hughes the lamp.

"Hold on——"

"We'll lift it easy with four," he says over his shoulder as he leaves the crypt. He heads down the ravine, skidding slightly on the frosty grass, then circles the Monument and climbs up the other side.

This time when he taps at the glass, it is Chief Tyrrell who opens. "Ready?"

Morrissey nods.

The detectives file out, pistols drawn. "Wait a minute, men," says Tyrrell. "It's so dark—tie your handkerchiefs round your arms so we can see not to shoot each other."

This procedure takes a little while. Tyrrell is still in his socks. Then they file round the corner of the Monument, Morrissey in the rear.

A shot, deafening.

"What the devil was that?"

A stammering voice. "Sorry, Chief, my cap went off."

"Get a move on!"

They break into a run. Somebody stumbles and falls with a yelp. When they reach the crypt, Tyrrell shoves the door open with his pistol butt. "Whoever's in there, come out!"

Dead silence.

"Just you come on out and surrender." After a long pause, he strikes a match and steps in. "Gone," he groans.

Ten days later, in the Hub, Mullen is tending bar in a clean apron and Hughes is dozing by the stove. "I still don't get it," says Mullen.

Hughes yawns.

"Tilden got three hundred thousand more votes than Hayes, am I right?"

"I keep telling you, there's more to it."

"No, but you can't tell me that three hundred thousand men don't matter."

"It's the Electoral College that matters," Hughes insists.

"Aw, this is all gum."

"If you'd pay attention—"

"It's bunkum, plumb and plain. More fellows voted for the Democrat."

"Maybe so," says Hughes, stroking his beard, "but Hayes is going to be President, and you owe me five dollars."

Mullen looks up as the door opens. "Morrissey, you scallywag!"

Hughes straightens in his chair. "We thought you'd run off to Canada."

"Naw, a patriot like me?" asks Morrissey, and they laugh.

But the fellow who has come into the saloon behind him draws and cocks his pistol at Hughes.

"What the hell—"

Mullen reaches for his gun but another man has stepped up behind him silently and has a revolver a foot from Mullen's head.

"You boys come along with the detectives, now," says Morrissey while they are being cuffed.

"Why, you piss-pot prick," Hughes says between his teeth.

Mullen's blue eyes are wide and crazy. "Morrissey? Did they catch you that night at the Monument?"

"Shut up, you dumb coot," groans Hughes. "Say nothing."

"No, but I need to know. Have they been leaning on you hard? Tell me you didn't give us up too easy."

Hughes twists in his cuffs to face his partner. "Don't you get it, you bootlicking idiot? This boy is all bull. He's been a bogus sham of a fake since the day he walked in here and bought you a drink."

Morrissey looks Mullen in the eye, one last time, and says, "Now, that's the truth."

The Body Swap

"Jim Morrissey" was the alias of one Lewis Cass Swegles (born in Michigan in 1849), a thief turned "roper" (undercover agent) for the Secret Service, who drew a wage of five dollars a day for his infiltration of a gang of counterfeiters who broke into Lincoln's tomb in 1876. This story owes a lot to Bonnie Stahlman Speer's *The Great Abraham Lincoln Hijack* (1997) and Thomas J. Craughwell's *Stealing Lincoln's Body* (2007).

Charged with conspiracy and larceny on Swegles's testimony, Terence Mullen and John Hughes faced up to eight years in Illinois's Joliet State Prison, but the jury sentenced them to just one year. After the trial, ten of the twelve jurymen sent a letter to the papers declaring that Swegles deserved a sentence of three years himself for entrapment of Hughes and Mullen. Soon after release, Hughes was sent back to Joliet for three years for passing counterfeit; Mullen, arrested on similar charges in 1880, informed against his former partner Big Jim Kinealy, who had sold Mullen's bar and vanished with the proceeds.

By 1880 Swegles was in Joliet himself, serving twelve years for burglary. He had a wife, Laura Baker (married back in 1872). He died in New York in 1896 at the age of forty-six.

JERSEY CITY
1877

THE GIFT

Mrs. Sarah Bell
177 3rd Street
Jersey City

March 5, 1877

I need to put my little one with you. Her name is
Lily May Bell, she is of one hundred per cent American
parentage. Her father John Bell died unexpected when
she was only three months old leaving me alone in the
world and I cannot supply her needs tho' not for want
of trying. I would work and take care of her but no
one will have me and her too, some say they would if
she was 2 or 3 years old. She is just from the breast,
her bowels have not been right for a long time. I have
cried and worried over her so much I think my milk
hurt her. I boarded Lily May out for some months so I
could work at dressmaking but she did not thrive, and
the woman said it might be the best in the end for a

fatherless mite. A neighbor told me in confidence that woman is no better than a baby farmer and doses them all stupid with syrup so I have taken Lily May out and can see no way except to throw myself on the mercy of your famous New York Society. Be kind to her for God's sake. You must not think that I neglected her. Do not be afraid of her face, it is nothing but an old ringworm. I will try hard to relieve you of her care as soon as ever can be.

Mrs. Sarah Bell
177 3rd Street
Jersey City

March 10, 1877

Thank you for your reply and for all your goodness. I hope Lily May does not "make strange" with the nurses for long but I suppose it is only to be expected. I do get some consolation from knowing I have done the best for her in my straitened circumstances. You say every child is assigned a place to sleep and a chair in the dining room which I am glad of, except that my baby cannot sit at table on her own yet so I hope there is someone to prop her up. I appreciate how busy the Rev. Brace and you all must be what with taking those unfortunates off the streets (and more swarming off every ship it seems), but if I may I will write from time to time to ask how mine is doing.

I am very sorry that I have nothing to send you but trust will come a day when I shall be able to pay you for all your trouble. I am in hopes of claiming Lily May before too long and God grant she will not recall a bit of it.

Please find herewith the form you sent.

This is to certify that I MRS. SARAH BELL *am the mother and only legal guardian of* LILY MAY BELL. *I hereby freely and of my own will agree for the New York Children's Aid Society to provide a home until* she *is of age or bind* her *out as the Managers may judge best. I hereby promise not to interfere in any way with the views and directions of the Managers.*

Mrs. Sarah Bell
177 3rd Street
Jersey City

April 2, 1877

I am relieved to hear about Lily May's bowels. You say a visit is not thought advisable, well once she is more settled in it might be a different story. I believe I could keep a hold of my feelings and not frighten her by giving way.

No one knows how awful it is to be separate from their child but a mother. You refer twice to "the orphans" but remember she is only a half, she has got one parent living. If I am spared and nothing prevents, the father of us all will permit me to have my little one back. Every night on my bended knees I pray for her.

Mrs. Sarah Bell
177 3rd Street
Jersey City

March 3, 1878

I have thought long and hard about what you say of the special trains going out west every week and the fresh air and placing out in farm homes. Institutions are confining to the young it is true and New York famously unhealthy. Do you pay these country women to take the children in? I fear that some would do it for mercenariness not kindness. Or perhaps they pay your Society, I have heard of such arrangements. But then that sounds like buying a horse at market. I am very much bewildered in my mind at the thought of my Lily May going off who knows where.

I planned by now to have put enough by to bring her back to Jersey with me but living is so dear. A home and friends is what I should wish for my little girl, at least until we can be reunited. I do recall the paper I signed last year but circumstances forced my hand. Do not take this as ingratitude, if I do not see her again I will never be worth anything on this earth. How far off do these trains go? If she is taken in by some family, do pass on my request that they will not change her name. Perhaps you will think me too particular but only consider how any mother would feel and you will excuse me.

In answer to your question there was never anything like that in my family or my husband's to my knowledge. Lily May is not two years old yet after all and my mother always said I was silent as the grave till I was three.

Mr. Bassett, Sheriff
Andes
New York

August 14, 1878

My wife and I have no children living, only one stillborn some twenty years back. Mrs. Bassett would like a girl between the ages of two and four, young enough to forget all that has gone before. No particular eye or hair color, except that if she is a foreigner she would stand out in Delaware County. So long as there is no hereditary taint we do not object to her being a foundling or illegitimate. In fact, we would prefer no relations. We do not particularly require the girl to be the student type, but want a happy-natured, responsive one and refined enough to take into our home. We would want to give her a High School education and if possible have her join the church choir.

I quite understand about no money changing hands, and signing the indenture. If a grievance arises can it be canceled?

We have gone to the hotel twice before, when orphan trains have come in, and enjoyed the songs and recitations, but never found anyone quite to our liking. There seemed a lot of older, rough-looking children. Mrs. Bassett would be afraid to take a boy, as harder to raise, and you never know. (It is not for farm work we want a child, unlike some fellow citizens we have seen squeezing boys' arms at the hotel.) I have talked to our doctor, who is on the town's Selection Committee. He said to write to the New York Society direct, and if you had a little girl who may answer our purposes, you might sew our request number right onto her hem, so she would not be given to anyone else.

*   *   *

Mr. Bassett, Sheriff
Andes
New York

November 3, 1878

My wife and I are so far much pleased with the child. At the hotel we took one good look at her, and then I nodded at Mrs. Bassett who could not speak, so I went up, and shook hands, and said, "You are going to be our little girl," She seemed queemish at first, but is getting used to the animals and no longer makes a face at the milk warm from the cow. She has a funny habit of keeping her arms on the table at meals; I suppose she learned it to prevent any other orphan from snatching her food.

We will keep her on trial for now, just in case. But barring serious misbehavior or disease, we mean to keep her and give her our name, Bassett I mean. Her first will be Mabel which keeps two of her old names—May Bell—in a hidden way as it were. She will have her room to herself, and more bonnets than she can wear. I can assure you we will take her to school and church and treat her as "no different."

*   *   *

Mrs. Sarah Bell
347 Grove Street
Jersey City

December 7, 1878

I could not give a proper answer to your letter last month as my heart was running over and remains the same. I am not ungrateful for this foster couple's Christianity but I could wish the circumstances otherwise. I write now just to inform you that I have changed my residence to the above and to ask to be informed the minute if anything should happen to my Lily as I have awful dreams. In the country between dogs and barb wire and rivers there is no knowing what could befall a little stranger.

Mr. Bassett, Sheriff
Andes
New York

February 6, 1879

Our Mabel is now one of the most content of children, and growing out of all her clothes. She has a rosy face and is most affectionate. She speaks more than before, though not quite clearly, but my wife can always make her out, so fears of feeblemindedness have been put to rest. She has quite forgotten her old name.

People here are civil, although I fear when she starts school, there will be a certain dose of meanness, as always among children. Such epithets as "bad blood" get thrown around with no thought for the hurt caused. Mrs. Bassett and I look on Mabel as quite our own, and could not love her more if she truly were. Your Agent can call on us anytime, we have nothing to hide.

I can appreciate that mothers do not like to part with their children, even to get them into much better situations. Can you assure us though that this Mrs. Bell will not be given our address? I have heard of cases where a woman abandons her child, and then lands up at the new home and makes scenes.

Mr. Bassett
Battle Creek
Iowa

November 3, 1879

Your last has, after some delay, reached us here in our new home. Please mark all future communications "Private," and do not use headed paper as nobody here knows of our connection with the Society. That in fact was one reason for our fresh start, though land and opportunity were others. It is mostly Germans round here, and no one seems to suspect Mabel is anything other than flesh of our flesh, a late gift from above. Keeping the secret we hope will shield her from the "pauper taint." She is a good girl and a talented singer, though her speech is still somewhat less plain than could be wished.

Thank you for sending the "adoption form," but on consideration we see no need for further fuss, and the risk of further publicity attendant on going through the courts. My wife holds to the principle that Mabel is our own already. We have made wills to provide for her future, all signed and sealed.

Mrs. Samuel Adams (Mrs. Sarah Bell as was)
697 2nd Avenue
Jersey City

April 23, 1880

I write to let you know of my change of fortune, as you will see from the above I am married again. We have "a good home" also (just as much as the couple who have got Lily May) and my husband Samuel who is in business is willing to welcome her into that home for which I thank God on bended knee as not every man would do the same.

If you have the slightest reservations you can send

one of your Agents to ask the neighbors what you like. I will always acknowledge your kindness and what these folks on the farm did in giving refuge to my Lily in a time of calamity but that time is over. Let me know how soon she can be brought back. I will hardly know my little one now!

Mr. Bassett
Battle Creek
Iowa

May 12, 1880

It shows heart that the mother has inquired, but there is no question of return like some parcel. My wife is upset the matter has been raised so cavalierlike, and says she will defy anyone to even talk of taking our girl away when we have already adopted her "in spirit." To my mind it is the day to day that makes a family, *de facto* if not *de jure*, and since your Society thought fit to give Mabel into our care, there have passed some five hundred days. She is going on four and we are all she knows in the world.

If as you say this woman has a new husband, why can't she make the best of it? Perhaps she will have more children with him, whereas Mrs. Bassett and self are past any chance of that.

I enclose a recent photograph so you can see how pleasant looking Mabel is turning out. I am in two minds about whether you ought to show the mother the picture. It might ease her to see how well the child is getting on, but then again it might increase the longing. On second thoughts, as it has the address of the studio on it, you had best not let her look at it.

Mrs. Samuel Adams
697 2nd Avenue
Jersey City

January 18, 1884

You may recognize my name as Mrs. Sarah Bell as I was before my present marriage. Since I wrote asking for my child Lily May near to four years ago and was refused, which I took very much to heart, circumstances have gone against Mr. Adams's ventures. But things are looking up again and we have moved to the above, which if you send an Agent as I asked you last time they will see is a gracious home fit for any young person. The Lord knows I am not the first mother to have been obliged to let go of a little one in a time of trouble but now I am in a position to keep house and reclaim my own Lily May.

I think of her all the time, at seven years old what

kind of life can it be in the wilds of Iowa when she was always nervous of a cat even? You say this couple treat her as "their own" but that is only make do and make believe as they must know in their heart of hearts. What is done can be undone if there is a will and a way. Surely if you pass this letter on to them so they can hear a mother's misery then they would have mercy if they are such good folks as you keep saying.

Mr. Bassett
Battle Creek
Iowa

September 24, 1885

I thank you for your two last. I apologize if mine had a "testy tone," only Mrs. Bassett was ill at the time, and sometimes it seems as if we will never be left at peace with our girl.

No, we do not think it advisable to enter into any kind of correspondence with this Adams woman (Bell as was), or encourage hopes of a visit. Is it not a queer thing for her to resume her talk of retrieving her child after all these years? I fear she has hopes of being paid off, as it is well known that the blood relations only kick up a fuss if they sniff money in it.

Mabel is so much our daughter, we look back on the

time before God gave her to us, and cannot imagine how we got through the lonesome days. She goes to school and Sunday School regularly and learns quickly. She regards tardiness almost as a crime. She is largish and has good health on the whole, though hardly what you would call rugged. She has not the least notion of being an adopted. My wife and I abide by "least said soonest mended."

Mr. Bassett
Battle Creek
Iowa

May 14, 1887

Enclosed please find the form completed as per and the fee of twenty-five dollars for the attorney. We never grudged the sum, it was only that my wife stood out against the intrusion and kept saying it smacked of having to pay for our beloved. But I have prevailed, since I live in terror of the mother turning up on our doorstep some day.

The NEW YORK CHILDREN'S AID SOCIETY hereby adopts to <u>Mr. and Mrs. Bassett</u> *an orphan named* <u>Mabel Bassett formerly Lily May Bell</u> *as our child, to keep, protect and treat as our own. We*

*covenant with said Society to provide said orphan with
suitable food, clothing, lodging and medical attendance,
in health and in sickness, and to instruct <u>her</u> adequately
in usefuless, as well as to advance and settle <u>her</u> in life
according as circumstances may permit.*

    *Witness our hands and seals this <u>12th</u> day of <u>May</u>
<u>1887.</u>*

Mrs. Sarah Bell
214 Beckman Avenue
Jersey City

February 20, 1889

    As you will see I am going by my old name again,
Mrs. Sarah Bell. I have suffered a divorce since I wrote
last but will likely be married again shortly to a much
more worthy man. Just now I can be reached at the
house of my father Mr. Joseph Prettyman, address
above, if you wish to send me any word.

    It seems I have known no luck in this world since
the day my first husband Mr. John Bell up and died on
me when Lily May my one and only was on my breast.
These ties are mysterious and unbreakable, you call her
"Mabel" but I will never use that name. Child stealing is what I call it, to send innocents by the trainload
into the most backward parts of the country and hand

them over to God knows who all, even when they have family living back East. All I asked was to take my Lily home with me and who better to love her than her own mother whose only crime was poverty?

It occurs to me now that my darling is past twelve. I wonder does she think of me at all or have her "folks" so-called kept her in the blackest ignorance of who she is.

Mrs. Sarah C. Mulkins
Davenport Center
New York

October 26, 1894

You may remember me as Mrs. Sarah Bell. I have been married again for some years to a good man called Mulkins and we have a very comfortable residence, see above. The other day I was thinking about my Lily May as I often and will always do and nothing can prevent a mother's heart from grieving, when I remembered that she comes of age next month. Surely at eighteen she should know the truth, that she has a loving mother who has never ceased from inquiring for her and never "abandoned" her as you cruelly put it, only gave her over for temporary safekeeping to preserve her from starvation. If she contacts your Society I trust you will in

Christian charity give her my address, you can do that much for all your cant of "legalities." Won't you please tell me how my Lily May is and whether I will be permitted to lay eyes on her again in this lifetime?

Mr. Bassett
Sioux City
Iowa

November 30, 1897

In response to your last several letters, I will tell you that Mabel was married this October 12th to a fine young man from Cedar County. We are much obliged to the Society for its concern over these long years, but now she is a grown woman and a wife, it seems to us her file should by rights be closed and as if it never were. You ask if she is ever to know who she is, which question Mrs. Bassett and I call impertinent, as she knows she is our beloved Mabel. We must insist that neither Mrs. Bell nor any other former connection shall ever learn anything about Mabel's whereabouts. We keep the papers locked up safe and whoever passes first, the other will burn them. We are not wealthy folk but this one gift we can leave to our girl and will.

The Gift

From 1853 to 1929, America saw a mass migration of a quarter of a million children on "Orphan Trains" (the Protestant phrase) or "Mercy Trains" or "Baby Cars" (the Catholic terms), which carried them from Eastern cities to the more rural and unpopulated West and Midwest, as well as to Canada and Mexico. This story is based on sketchy notes, from the ledgers of the New York Children's Aid Society, on the Society's correspondence with Lily May Bell's birth mother and adoptive parents (www.iagenweb.org/iaorphans/riders/bell.shtml). Some phrases are borrowed from letters in the archives of the New York Foundling Hospital, quoted in Lisa Lipkin, "The Child I've Left Behind," *New York Times Magazine,* May 19, 1996.

Many birth parents did manage to get their children back years later, but not Lily May Bell's mother. The child became Mabel Bassett, then changed her name again, on marriage to a local man, William H. Filson, in 1897. At the time of the 1900 census, the Filsons were still living in Tipton, Cedar County, Iowa, with their baby daughter. By 1910, they were divorced, and Mabel and their two Iowa-born children (Freda and Florence) were living with her parents in Los Angeles; the 1910 census lists Mabel as "daughter (adopted)" of Adam(s) and Elven [Evelyn? Elvira?] Bassett and gives her birth as New York, 1880. The date is about three years late, but the place is right; had her parents told her by then that she was adopted, or did they whisper the secret to the census taker? Ten years later, the 1920 census shows Mabel still in L.A., but re-married, this time to a Nelson Middleton, with Florence and Freda (now a university student) listed as his "daughters" (no qualify-ing "adopted" this time). By 1930 Mabel and Nelson were living with Freda and her eight-year-old daughter, Evelyn Friel; perhaps Freda had been widowed, or divorced like her mother, or had the child out of wedlock. Finally, the California Death Index gives Ma-bel Bassett Middleton a birth of March 5, 1879, New York, and a death of January 23, 1948, L.A. If we accept the Children's Aid Society's record that she was probably born in 1876, she lived to be about seventy-one.

ARRIVALS AND
AFTERMATHS

CAPE COD
1639

THE LOST SEED

In this world we are as seed scattered from God's hand. Some fall on the fat soil and thrive. Some fall among thorns and are choked as they grow. Some fall on hard ground, and their roots get no purchase, for the bitter rocks lie all around.

I, Richard Berry, make this record in the margins of the Good Book for those who come after, lest our plantation fail and all trace of our endeavors be wiped from the earth. Shielded by the Lord's arm, our ship has traveled safe across the ocean through all travails, to make landfall at the colony of Plymouth. Today we stretched our legs on land again. The snow reaches our knees. We never saw stuff like this before. It is bright as children's teeth and squeaks underfoot.

On the first day of June came the quake. So powerful is the mighty hand of the Lord, it makes both the earth and the sea to shake. Many of our thatched huts fell down.

But we and the settlers who came before us keep faith with our Maker and our mission. We go on hacking ourselves a space in the wilderness of Cape Cod: our settlement is to be called Yarmouth. The mosquitoes bite us till we are striped with blood. May we cast off the old sins of England like dust from our boots.

I have written nothing in this book for a time, being much occupied with laboring for the good of the Lord and this plantation. We have made new laws, and set down on paper the liberties of all freemen. The Indians have shown us how to bury dead fish with our seeds to sweeten the soil. We have sold them guns.

I am still unmarried. I thought on Sarah White but she laughs overmuch.

Of late I have been troubled by a weakness of spirit. I dwell on my mother and father and come near to weeping, for I will never see them again in this life. But I must remember that those who till the soil beside me are my brethren.

There are few enough of our congregation aboveground. Edward Preston lost his wife this past month, and so did Teague Joanes, a godly man whose field lies next to mine. For ye know not the hour. There are others in Yarmouth who seek to stir up division like mud in a creek. At Meeting they grasp at privilege and make much of themselves. But our dissensions must be thrust aside. If we do not help each other, who will help us? We are all sojourners in a strange land: we must lend aid, and stand guard against attack, and carry our faith like a precious stone. We hear of other plantations where there is not a Christian left alive.

Our court sentenced Seb Mitchel to be fined three pounds for his unseemly and blasphemous speeches. He spoke against his Maker for taking all three of Seb's children. He will have to give his hog to pay the fine.

Our numbers in Yarmouth are increased with the coming of ships, yet I dislike these incomers, who are all puffed up and never think of our sweat that built this town. I pray they be not like the seed that springs up quick and eager but is soon parched and blasted by the noonday sun.

Sarah White is married to Hugh Norman these two months past. She is lightsome of countenance and speech. She forgets the saying of the Apostle, that wives should submit. If she does not take care, her behavior will be spoken of at Meeting. I went by her house the other day, and she was singing a song. I could not make out the words, but it was no hymn.

These days some play while others work. Things that are lawful in moderation, whether archery or foot-racing, tobacco or ale, are become traps for the weak. Each man goes his own way, it seems; there is little concord or meekness of spirit. I remind my brethren that we are not separate, one from the other. Another bad winter could extinguish us. In this rough country we stand together or we fall.

God has not yet granted me a helpmeet. I look about me diligently at the sisters in our plantation, but some are shrewish, and others have a barren look about them, or a limp, or a cast in the eye.

In the first days, I remember, we were all one family in the Lord. But now each household shuts its doors at night. Every man looks to his own wife and his own children. I think on the first days, when there was great fellowship, through all trials.

Last night there was a snow so heavy that the whole plantation was made one white. I stood in my door and saw some flakes as wide as my hand, that came down faster than the others. Every flake falls alone, and yet on the ground they are all one.

Twice in these last months a woman has come big-bellied to be married, and she and the man put a shame-face on and paid their fine to the court, but it is clear think little of their sin.

Our court sentenced Joan Younge's master to pay her fine of two pounds, for she was rude to her mistress on the Lord's day and blocked her ears when the Bible was read, and the master should have kept her under firm governance. I would have had the girl whipped down to the bone.

Teague Joanes is the only man now who says more to me than yea or nay.

At sunset most evenings I meet him where our cornfields join. He tells me that though marriage be our duty, it brings much grief, and from the hour a child is born his father is never without fear.

Hugh Norman's daughter was found in the well, five years old. I went by their house and offered a word of succor to the mother, Sarah, but she would not leave off howling like a beast. One of John Vincent's daughters was there.

Good news on the last ship. King Charles has been cast down for his Popish wickedness. Men of conscience govern England. Heathenish festivities no longer defile the name of the Lord, and there is no more Christmas.

Here we work till the light fails. We have indentured men, some blacks among them, to hoe the land, but still too much of the crop is lost in the weeds, and strangled in rankness.

Mary Vincent is fifteen, and comely, but not overmuch.

Our court found Nathaniel Hatch and his sister Lydia Hatch guilty of unclean practices. They have strayed so far from the path, they are sheep who cannot be brought home. He is to be banished to the south and she to the north. We are not to break bread with them, or so much as throw them a crust. If we happen to pass either of them in the road, we are to turn our faces away. If either tries to speak to any of our community, we are to stop up our ears. No other town in Plymouth, or any other Christian plantation, will take in a cast-out.

I gave my view in Meeting that the pair should have been put to death for their incest, as a sign to waverers. (And after all, to be cast out is itself a sort of death, for who would wish to roam this wilderness alone?) It has seemed to me for some time that our laws are too soft. If any man go after strange flesh, or children, or fowl or other beasts, even if the deed be not accomplished, it should be death. If any man act upon himself so as to spill his seed on the ground, it should be exile, at least. For the seed is most precious in these times and must not be lost.

I spoke to Mary Vincent's father, and he was not opposed, but the girl would not have me.

I am a fruitless man. My grievous sins of pride and hardheartedness have made me to bury my coin in the ground, like the bad servant in the parable. I have begot no children to increase our plantation. All I can do is work.

There is talk of making a law against the single life, so that every unmarried man or woman would have to go and live in some godly family. But what house would take me in?

Nathaniel Hatch is rumored to be living still in the woods to the south of Yarmouth. I wonder if he has repented of his filth. Even if the wolves have spared him, he has no people now. As for his sister, no one has set eyes on her.

Mary Vincent is to marry Benjamin Hammon.

My face is furrowed like a cornfield. The ice leaves its mark, and the burning summer turns all things brown. But I will cast off vanity. The body is but the husk that is tossed aside in the end.

Benjamin Hammon said to Teague Joanes that Sarah Norman told his wife I was an old killjoy.

It matters not.

Sin creeps around like a fog in the night. Too many of us forget to be watchful. Too many have left their doors open for the Tempter to slip in. I puzzle over it as I lie on my bed in the darkness, but I cannot tell why stinking lusts and things fearful to name should arise so commonly among us. It may be that our strict laws stop up the channel of wickedness, but it searches everywhere and at last breaks out worse than before.

I consider it my pressing business to stand sentry. Where vice crawls out of the shadows, I shine a light on it. Death still seizes so many of our flock each winter, we cannot spare a single soul among the survivors. Better I should anger my neighbor than stand by and watch the Tempter pluck up his soul as the eagle fastens on the lamb. Better I should be spurned and despised, and feel myself to be entirely alone on this earth, than that I should relinquish my holy labor. They call me killjoy, but let them tell me this, what business have we with joy? What time have we to spare for joy, and what have we done to deserve it?

The Lord has entered into the Temple and the cleansing has begun. Let the godless tremble, but the clean of heart rejoice.

This day by my information charges were laid against Sarah Norman, together with Mary Hammon, fifteen years old and newly a wife, the more her shame. I testified to what I witnessed. With my own eyes I saw them, as I stood by Hugh Norman's window in the heat of the day. His wife and Benjamin Hammon's were lying on the one bed together. They were naked as demons, and there was not a hand-span between their bodies.

It is time now to put our feet to the spades to dig up evil and all its roots.

But already there is weakening. Our court was prevailed upon to let the girl go, with only an admonition, on account of her youth. The woman's case has been held over until the weight of business allows it to be heard. But I have faith she will be brought to judgment at last after all these years of giddiness. In the meantime, Hugh Norman has sworn he will put her and her children out of his house. I gave my belief that she should be cast out of Yarmouth.

Teague Joanes came to my house last night after dark, a thing he has never done before. He said, was it not likely the woman and the girl were only comforting each other when I saw them through the window, and what soul did not need some consolation in these hard times? I reminded him that consolation was not to be sought nor found in this life, but the next. He would have prevailed upon me to show mercy, as the Father did to his Prodigal. But I gave my belief that by their transgression Sarah Norman and Mary Hammon have strayed far beyond the reach of mercy.

Then he asked me a curious thing, did I never feel lonely? In the depth of winter, say, when the snow fills up all the pathways.

I told him I never did. But this was akin to a lie.

Teague said he could not believe I was such a hard man. I gave him no answer, for my thoughts were all confounded. Then he said at any rate he would not part with me on bad terms, and came up to me and held on to me, and his leg lay against my leg.

All that was last night. And today charges were laid by my information against Teague Joanes for an attempt at sodomy.

These are bitter times. The wind of opposition blows full in my face, but I must not turn aside, for fear of my soul.

At last our court found Sarah Norman guilty of lewd behavior with Mary Hammon, but sentenced her merely to make a public acknowledgment on the Lord's day following. She lives now in a mud hut on the edge of our plantation, and her children with her, as Hugh Norman has taken ship back to England. With my own eyes I have seen some of the brethren stop to speak with her on the road. I ask why she has not been exiled, and there is none will answer me.

The case against Teague Joanes has not yet been heard. He is well liked among those who are deceived by a show of friendliness and the Tempter's own sweet smile. Many whisper that the charges should be struck out as unfounded. No one says a word to me these days. But I know what I know.

Our paths crossed on the Lord's day, and he spat on my back.

I am not a dreaming man, but last night the most dreadful sight was shown to me. I saw Teague Joanes and Sarah Norman consorting uncleanly on a bed, the man behind the woman, turning the natural use to that which is against nature, and laughing all the while.

And when I woke I knew this was no fancy but a true vision, granted me by the Lord, so that with the eyes of sleep I could witness what is hidden in the light of day. So I walked to the court and laid charges against them both for sodomy.

The clerk did not want to write down my dream. So I took him by the collar and I asked, would he wrestle with God's own angel?

In the whole town there is none who will greet me. I hear the slurs they cast upon me as I go down the street.

I work in my own field, though these days my bones creak like dead trees. I keep my head down if ever someone passes by. I wait for the court to hear my evidence. I must stand fast.

Today I was called to the court. I stepped out my door, and over my head were hanging icicles as thick as my fist and sharp like swords of glass.

There in the court were Teague Jones and Sarah Norman and Benjamin Hammon and his wife Mary together with many others, the whole people of Plymouth. And I read on their faces that they were my enemies and God's.

At first I spoke up stoutly and told of the wickedness that

is spreading through this plantation, and of the secrets that hide in the folds of men's hearts. And then Teague Joanes stood up and shouted out that I was a madman and that I had no heart.

It was quiet for a moment, a quietness I have never heard before.

Then I was asked over and over again about what I had seen, and what I had imagined, and what I knew for sure. But I could not answer. I felt a terrible spinning. All I could think on was the evening Teague Joanes walked in my door. Not of the words he spoke, but the way he stood there, looking in my eyes as few know how to in these times. The way he laid his arms around me, fearless, and pressed me to him, as one brother to another. And all of a sudden I remembered the treacherous stirring between us, the swelling of evil, and I knew whose body began it.

So I said out very loud in front of the whole court that I had perjured myself and that I withdrew the charges and that I was damned for all time. And when I walked to the door, the people moved out of my way so as not to touch me.

I went across the fields for fear of meeting any human creature on the road. And it seemed to me the snow was like a face, for its crust is an image of perfection, but underneath is all darkness and slime. And I wept, a thing I have not done since I was a child, and the water turned to ice on my cheeks.

The Lost Seed

The story of Richard Berry comes from a cluster of terse legal records in *Records of the Colony of New Plymouth*, edited by N. B. Shurtleff (1855). A resident of Yarmouth (founded 1639, one of the twenty-one towns of Plymouth Plantation on Cape Cod), in 1649 Berry started accusing neighbors—Sarah White Norman, Mary Vincent Hammon, Teague Joanes—of various sex crimes. The following year, in a volte-face, Berry confessed to having borne false witness against Joanes and was publicly whipped. Three years on, Berry, Joanes, and others were ordered to "part their uncivil living together."

Kenneth Borris's *Same-Sex Desire in the English Renaissance* (2004) digs up a few more facts about Berry's targets. Sarah's husband never took her and the children back, but went off to England with an inheritance, which he promptly wasted. Mary and Vincent Hammon, however, had a number of children before he died in 1703.

In 1659 one "Richard Beare" was found guilty of "filthy obscene practices" and banished from the colony; this seems likely to be a variant spelling for the same old troublemaker.

VACHERIE, LOUISIANA
1839

VANITAS

This afternoon I was so stone bored, I wrote something on a scrap of paper and put it in a medicine bottle, sealed it up with the stub of a candle. I was sitting on the levee; I tossed the bottle as far as I could (since I throw better than girls should) and the Mississippi took it, lazily. If you got in a boat here by the Duparc-Locoul Plantation, and didn't even row or raise a sail, the current would take you down fifty miles of slow curves to New Orleans in the end. That's if you didn't get tangled up in weed.

What I wrote on the scrap was *Au secours!* Then I put the date, *3 juillet 1839*. The Americans if drowning or in other trouble call out, *Help!*, which doesn't capture the attention near as much, it's more like a little sound a puppy would make. The bottle was green glass with *Poison* down one side. I wonder who'll fish it out of the brown water, and what will that man or woman or child make of my message? Or will the medicine bottle float right through the city, out into the Gulf of Mexico, and my scribble go unread till the end of time?

It was a foolish message, and a childish thing to do. I know that; I'm fifteen, which is old enough that I know when I'm being a child. But I ask you, how's a girl to pass an after-noon as long and scalding as this one? I stare at the river in hopes of seeing a boat go by, or a black gum tree with muddy roots. A week ago I saw a blue heron swallow down a wrig-gling snake. Once in a while a boat will have a letter for us, a boy attaches it to the line of a very long fishing rod and flicks it over to our pier. I'm supposed to call a nègre to untie the letter and bring it in; Maman hates when I do it myself. She says I'm a gateur de nègres, like Papa, we spoil them with soft handling. She always beats them when they steal things, which they call only *taking*.

I go up the pecan alley toward the Maison, and through the gate in the high fence that's meant to keep the animals out. Passers-by always know a Creole house by the yellow and red, not like the glaring white American ones. Everything on our Plantation is yellow and red—not just the houses but the stables, the hospital, and the seventy slave cabins that stretch back like a village for three miles, with their vegetable gardens and chicken pens.

I go in the Maison now, not because I want to, just to get away from the bam-bam-bam of the sun on the back of my neck. I step quietly past Tante Fanny's room, because if she hears me she might call me in for some more lessons. My parents are away in New Orleans doing business; they never take me. I've never been anywhere, truth to tell. My brother, Emile, has been in the Lycée Militaire in Bordeaux for five years already, and when he graduates, Maman says perhaps we will all go on a voyage to France. By all, I don't mean Tante Fanny, because she never leaves her room, nor her husband, Oncle Louis, who lives in New Orleans and does business for us, nor Oncle Flagy and Tante Marcelite, quiet sorts who prefer to stay here always and see to the nègres, the field ones and the house ones. It will be just Maman and Papa and I who go to meet Emile in France. Maman is the head of the Famille ever since Grandmère Nannette Prud'Homme retired; we Creoles hand the reins to the smartest child, male or female (unlike the Americans, whose women are too feeble to run things). But Maman never really wanted to oversee the family enterprise, she says if her brothers Louis and Flagy were more useful she and Papa could have gone back to la belle France and stayed there. And then I would have been born a French mademoiselle. "Creole" means born of French stock, here in Louisiana, but Maman prefers to call us French. She says France is like nowhere else in the world, it's all things gracious and fine and civilized, and no sacrés nègres about the place.

I pass Millie on the stairs, she's my maid and sleeps on the floor of my room but she has to help with everything else as well. She's one of Pa Philippe's children, he's very old (for a nègre), and has VPD branded on both cheeks from when he used to run away, that stands for Veuve Prud'Homme Duparc. It makes me shudder a little to look at the marks. Pa Philippe can whittle anything out of cypress with his little knife: spoons, needles, pipes. Since Maman started our breeding program, we have more small nègres than we know what to do with, but Millie's the only one as old as me. "Allo, Millie," I say, and she says, "Mam'zelle Aimée," and grins back but forgets to curtsy.

"Aimée" means beloved. I've never liked it as a name. It seems it should belong to a different kind of girl.

Where I am bound today is the attic. Though it's hotter than the cellars, it's the one place nobody else goes. I can lie on the floor and chew my nails and fall into a sort of dream. But today the dust keeps making me sneeze. I'm restless, I can't settle. I try a trick my brother, Emile, once taught me, to make yourself faint. You breathe in and out very fast while you count to a hundred, then stand against the wall and press as hard as you can between your ribs. Today I do it twice, and I feel odd, but that's all; I've never managed to faint as girls do in novels.

I poke through some wooden boxes but they hold nothing except old letters, tedious details of imports and taxes and engagements and deaths of people I never heard of. At the back there's an old-fashioned sheepskin trunk, I've tried to open it before. Today I give it a real wrench and the top comes up. Ah, now here's something worth looking at. Real silk, I'd say, as yellow as butter, with layers of tulle underneath, and an embroidered girdle. The sleeves are huge and puffy, like sacks of rice. I slip off my dull blue frock and try it on over my shift. The skirt hovers, the sleeves bear me up so I seem to float over the splinters and dust of the floorboards. If only I had a looking glass up here. I know I'm short and homely, with a fat throat, and my hands and feet are too big, but in this sun-colored dress I feel halfway to beautiful. Grandmère Nannette, who lives in her Maison de Reprise across the yard and is descended from Louis XV's own physician, once said that like her I was pas jolie but at least we had our skin, un teint de roses. Maman turns furious if I go out without my sunhat or a parasol, she says if I get freckled like some Cajun farm girl, how is she supposed to find me a good match? My stomach gets tight at the thought of a husband, but it won't happen before I'm sixteen, at least. I haven't even become a woman yet, Maman says, though I'm not sure what she means.

I dig in the trunk. A handful of books; the collected poetry of Lord Byron, and a novel by Victor Hugo called *Notre-Dame de Paris*. More dresses—a light violet, a pale peach—and light shawls like spiders' webs, and, in a heavy traveling case, some strings of pearls, with rings rolled up in a piece of black velvet. The bottom of the case lifts up, and there I find the strangest thing. It must be from France. It's a sort of bracelet—a thin gold chain—with trinkets dangling from it. I've never seen such perfect little oddities. There's a tiny silver locket that refuses to open; a gold cross, a monkey (grimacing), a minute kneeling angel, a pair of ballet slippers. A tiny tower of some sort, a snake, a crouching tiger (I recognize his toothy roar from the encyclopedia), and a machine with miniature wheels that go round and round; I think this must be a locomotive, like we use to haul cane to our sugar mill. But the one I like best, I don't know why, is a gold key. It's so tiny, I can't imagine what door or drawer or box in the world it might open.

Through the window, I see the shadows are getting longer; I must go down and show myself, or there'll be a fuss. I pack the dresses back into the trunk, but I can't bear to give up the bracelet. I manage to open its narrow catch, and fasten the chain around my left arm above the elbow, where no one will see it under my sleeve. I mustn't show it off, but I'll know it's there; I can feel the little charms moving against my skin, pricking me.

"*Vanitas,*" says Tante Fanny. "The Latin word for—?"

"Vanity," I guess.

"A word with two meanings. Can you supply them?"

"A, a desire to be pretty, or finely dressed," I begin.

She nods, but corrects me: "Self-conceit. The holding of too high an opinion of one's beauty, charms or talents. But it also means futility," she says, very crisp. "Worthlessness. What is done *in vain*. Vanitas paintings illustrate the vanity of all human wishes. Are you familiar with Ecclesiastes, chapter one, verse two?"

I hesitate. I scratch my arm through my sleeve, to feel the little gold charms.

My aunt purses her wide mouth. Though she is past fifty now, with the sallow look of someone who never sees the sun, and always wears black, you can tell that she was once a beauty. "*Vanity of vanities, saith the Preacher, vanity of vanities,*" she quotes; "*all is vanity.*"

That's Cousine Eliza on the wall behind her mother's chair, in dark oils. In the picture she looks much older than sixteen to me. She is sitting in a chair with something in her left hand, I think perhaps a handkerchief; has she been crying? Her white dress has enormous sleeves, like clouds; above them, her shoulders slope prettily. Her face is creamy and perfectly oval, her eyes are dark, her hair is coiled on top of her head like a strange plum cake. Her lips are together, it's a perfect mouth, but it looks so sad. Why does she look so sad?

"In this print here," says Tante Fanny, tapping the portfolio in her lap with one long nail (I don't believe she ever cuts them), "what does the hourglass represent?"

I bend to look at it again. A grim man in seventeenth-century robes, his desk piled with objects. "Time?" I hazard.

"And the skull?"

"Death."

"Très bien, Aimée."

I was only eight when my uncle and aunt came back from France, with—among their copious baggage—Cousine Eliza in a lead coffin. She'd died of a fever. Papa came back from Paris right away, with the bad news, but the girl's parents stayed on till the end of the year, which I thought strange. I was not allowed to go to the funeral, though the cemetery of St. James is only ten miles upriver. After the funeral was the last time I saw my Oncle Louis. He's never come back to the Plantation since, and for seven years Tante Fanny hasn't left her room. She's shut up like a saint; she spends hours kneeling at her little prie-dieu, clutching her beads, thumping her chest. Millie brings all her meals on trays, covered to keep off the rain or the flies. Tante Fanny also sews and writes to her old friends and relations in France and Germany. And, of course, she teaches me. Art and music, French literature and handwriting, religion and etiquette (or, as she calls it, les convenances and comme il faut). She can't supervise my piano practice, as the instrument is in the salon at the other end of the house, but she leaves her door open, when I'm playing, and strains her ears to catch my mistakes.

This morning instead of practicing I was up in the attic again, and I saw a ghost, or at least I thought I did. I'd taken all the dresses out of the old sheepskin trunk, to admire and hold against myself; I'd remembered to bring my hand mirror up from my bedroom, and if I held it at arm's length, I could see myself from the waist up, at least. I danced like a gypsy, like the girl in *Notre-Dame de Paris,* whose beauty wins the heart of the hideous hunchback.

When I pulled out the last dress—a vast white one that crinkled like paper—what was revealed was a face. I think I cried out; I know I jumped away from the trunk. When I made myself go nearer, the face turned out to be made of something hard and white, like chalk. It was not a bust, like the one downstairs of poor Marie Antoinette. This had no neck, no head; it was only the smooth, pitiless mask of a girl, lying among a jumble of silks.

I didn't recognize her at first; I can be slow. My heart was beating loudly in a sort of horror. Only when I'd sat for some time, staring at those pristine, lidded eyes, did I realize that the face was the same as the one in the portrait of Cousine Eliza, and the white dress I was holding was the dress she wore in the painting. These were all her clothes that I was playing with, it came to me, and the little gold bracelet around my arm had to be hers too. I tried to take it off and return it to the trunk, but my fingers were so slippery I couldn't undo the catch. I wrenched at it, and there was a red line around my arm; the little charms spun.

Tante Fanny's room is stuffy; I can smell the breakfast tray that waits for Millie to take it away. "Tante Fanny," I say now, without preparation, "why does Cousine Eliza look so sad?"

My aunt's eyes widen violently. Her head snaps.

I hear my own words too late. What an idiot, to make it sound as if her daughter's ghost was in the room with us! "In the picture," I stammer, "I mean in the picture, she looks sad."

Tante Fanny doesn't look round at the portrait. "She was dead," she says, rather hoarse.

This can't be right. I look past her. "But her eyes are open."

My aunt lets out a sharp sigh and snaps her book shut. "Do you know the meaning of the word 'posthumous'?"

"Eh..."

"After death. The portrait was commissioned and painted in Paris in the months following my daughter's demise."

I stare at it again. But how? Did the painter prop her up somehow? She doesn't look dead, only sorrowful, in her enormous, ice-white silk gown.

"Eliza did not model for it," my aunt goes on, as if explaining something to a cretin. "For the face, the artist worked from a death mask." She must see the confusion in my eyes. "A sculptor pastes wet plaster over the features of a corpse. When it hardens he uses it as a mold, to make a perfect simulacrum of the face."

That's it. That's what scared me, up in the attic this morning: Eliza's death mask. When I look back at my aunt, there's been a metamorphosis. Tears are chasing down her papery cheeks. "Tante Fanny—"

"Enough," she says, her voice like mud. "Leave me."

I don't believe my cousin—my only cousin, the beautiful Eliza, just sixteen years old—died of a fever. Louisiana is a hellhole for fevers of all kinds, that's why my parents sent Emile away to Bordeaux. It's good for making money, but not for living, that's why Napoleon sold it so cheap to the Americans thirty-six years ago. So how could it have happened that Eliza grew up here on the Duparc-Locoul Plantation, safe and well, and on her trip to Paris—that pearly city, that apex of civilization—she succumbed to a fever? I won't believe it, it smells like a lie.

I'm up in the attic again, but this time I've brought the Bible. My brother, Emile, before he went away to France, taught me how to tell fortunes with the Book and Key. In those days we used an ugly old key we'd found in the cellars, but now I have a better one; the little gold one that hangs on my bracelet. (Eliza's bracelet, I should say.) What you do is, you open the Bible to the Song of Solomon, pick any verse you like, and read it aloud. If the key goes clockwise, it's saying yes to the verse, and vice versa. Fortune-telling is a sin when gypsies or conjurers do it, like the nègres making their nasty gris-gris to put curses on each other, but it can't be wrong if you use the Good Book. The Song of Solomon is the most puzzling bit of the Bible but it's my favorite. Sometimes it seems to be a man speaking, and sometimes a woman; she says *I am black but comely,* but she can't be a nègre, surely. They adore each other, but at some points it sounds as if they are brother and sister.

My first question for the Book today is, did Cousine Eliza die a natural death? I pull the bracelet down to my wrist, and I hold all the other little charms still, letting only the key dangle. I shake my hand as I recite the verse I've chosen, one that reminds me of Eliza: *Thy cheeks are comely with rows of jewels, thy neck with chains of gold.* When my hand stops moving, the key swings, most definitely anticlockwise. I feel a thrill all the way down in my belly. So! Not a natural death; as I suspected.

What shall I ask next? I cross my legs, to get more comfortable on the bare boards, and study the Book. A verse gives me an idea. Was she—is it possible—she was murdered? Not a night goes by in a great city without a cry in the dark, I know that much. *The watchmen that went about the city found me,* I whisper, *they smote me, they wounded me.* I shake my wrist, and the key dances, but every which way; I can't tell what the answer is. I search for another verse. Here's one: *Every man hath his sword upon his thigh because of fear in the night.* What if...I rack my imagination. What if two young Parisian gallants fought a duel over her, after glimpsing her at the opera, and Eliza died of the shock? I chant the verse, my voice rising now, because no one will hear me up here. I wave my hand in the air, and when I stop moving, the key continues to swing, counterclockwise. No duel, then; that's clear.

But what if she had a lover, a favorite among all the gentlemen of France who were vying for the hand of the exquisite Creole maiden? What if he was mad with jealousy and strangled her, locking his hands around her long pale neck rather than let Tante Fanny and Oncle Louis take her back to Louisiana? *For love is strong as death; jealousy is cruel as the grave,* I croon, and my heart is thumping, I can feel the wet break out under my arms, in the secret curls there. I've forgotten to wave my hand. When I do it, the key swings straight back and forward, like the clapper of a bell. Like the thunderous bells in the high cathedral of Notre-Dame de Paris. Is that an answer? Not jealousy, then, or not exactly; some other strange passion? Somebody killed Eliza, whether they meant to or not, I remind myself; somebody is to blame for the sad eyes in that portrait. For Tante Fanny walled up in her stifling room, and Oncle Louis who never comes home.

I can't think of any more questions about Eliza; my brain is fuzzy. Did she suffer terribly? I can't find a verse to ask that. How can I investigate a death that happened eight years ago, all the way across the ocean, when I'm only a freckled girl who's never left the Plantation? Who'll listen to my questions, who'll tell me anything?

I finish by asking the Book something for myself. Will I ever be pretty, like Eliza? Will these dull and round features ever bloom into perfect conjunction? Will I grow a face that will take me to France, that will win me the love of a French gentleman? Or will I be stuck here for the rest of my life, my mother's harried assistant and perhaps her successor, running the Plantation and the wine business and the many complex enterprises that make up the wealth of the Famille Duparc-Locoul? That's too many questions. Concentrate, Aimée. Will I be pretty when I grow up? *Behold, thou art fair, my love,*

I murmur, as if to make it so; *behold, thou art fair*. But then something stops me from shaking my hand, making the key swing. Because what if the answer is no?

I stoop over the trunk and take out the death mask, as I now know it's called. I hold it very carefully in my arms, and I lie down beside the trunk. I look into the perfect white oval of my cousin's face, and lay it beside mine. *Eliza, Eliza*. I whisper my apologies for disturbing her things, for borrowing her bracelet, with all its little gold and silver trinkets. I tell her I only want to know the truth of how she died so her spirit can be at rest. My cheek is against her cool cheek, my nose aligns itself with hers. The plaster smells of nothing. I set my dry lips to her smooth ones.

"Millie," I ask, when she's buttoning up my dress this morning, "you remember my Cousine Eliza?"

The girl makes a little humming sound that could mean yes, no, or maybe. That's one of her irritating habits. "You must," I say. "My beautiful cousin who went away to Paris. They say she died of a fever."

This time the sound she makes is more like *hmph*.

I catch her eye, its milky roll. Excitement rises in my throat. "Millie," I say, too loud, "have you ever heard anything about that?"

"What would I hear, Mam'zelle Aimée?"

"Oh, go on! I know you house nègres are always gossiping. Did you ever hear tell of anything strange about my cousin's death?"

Millie's glance slides to the door. I step over there and shut it. "Go on. You can speak freely."

She shakes her head, very slowly.

"I know you know something," I say, and it comes out too fierce. Governing the nègres is an art, and I don't have it; I'm too familiar, and then too cross. Today, watching Millie's purple mouth purse, I resort to a bribe. "I tell you what, I might give you a present. What about one of these little charms?" Through my sleeve, I tug the gold bracelet down to my wrist. I make the little jewels shake and spin in front of Millie's eyes. "What about the tiger, would you like that one?" I point him out, because how would she know what a tiger looks like? "Or maybe these dance slippers. Or the golden cross, which Jesus died on?" I don't mention the key, because that's my own favorite.

Millie looks hungry with delight. She's come closer; her fingers are inches away from the dancing trinkets.

I tuck the bracelet back under my wrist ruffle. "Tell me!"

She crosses her arms and leans in close to my ear. She smells a little ripe, but not too bad. "Your cousine?"

"Yes."

"Your oncle and tante killed her."

I shove the girl away, the flat of my hand against her collarbone. "How dare you!"

She gives a luxurious shrug. "All I say is what I hear."

"Hear from whom?" I demand. "Your Pa Philippe, or your Ma?" Millie's mother works the hoe-gang, she's strong as a man. "What would they know of my family's affairs?"

Millie is grinning as she shakes her head. "From your tante."

"Tante Marcelite? She'd never say such a thing."

"No, no. From your Tante Fanny."

I'm so staggered I have to sit down. "Millie, you know it's the blackest of sins to lie," I remind her. "I think you must have made up this story. You're saying that my Tante Fanny told you—you—that she and Oncle Louis murdered Eliza?"

Millie's looking sullen now. "I don't make up nothing. I go in and out of that dusty old room five times a day with trays, and sometimes your tante is praying or talking to herself, and I hear her."

"But this is ridiculous." My voice is shaking. "Why would—what reason could they possibly have had for killing their own daughter?" I run through the plots I invented up in the attic. Did Eliza have a French lover? Did she *give herself* to him and fall into ruin? Could my uncle and aunt have murdered her, to save the Famille from shame? "I won't hear any more of such stuff."

The nègre has the gall to put her hand out, cupped for her reward.

"You may go now," I tell her, stepping into my shoes.

Next morning, I wake up in a foul temper. My head starts hammering as soon as I lift it off the pillow. Maman is expected back from New Orleans today. I reach for my bracelet on the little table beside my bed and it's gone.

"Millie?" But she's not there, on the pallet at the foot of my bed; she's up already. She's taken my bracelet. I never mentioned giving her more than one little trinket; she couldn't have misunderstood me. Damn her for a thieving little nègre.

I could track her down in the kitchen behind the house,

or in the sewing room with Tante Marcelite, working on the slave clothes, or wherever she may be, but no. For once, I'll see to it that the girl gets punished for her outrageous impudence.

I bide my time; I do my lessons with Tante Fanny all morning. My skin feels greasy, I've a bouton coming out on my chin; I'm a martyr to pimples. This little drum keeps banging away in the back of my head. And a queasiness, too; a faraway aching. What could I have eaten to put me in such a state?

When the boat arrives I don't rush down to the pier; my mother hates such displays. I sit in the shady gallery and wait. When Maman comes to find me, I kiss her on both cheeks. "Perfectly well," I reply. (She doesn't like to hear of symptoms, unless one is seriously ill.) "But that dreadful brat Millie has stolen a bracelet from my room." As I say it, I feel a pang, but only a little one. Such a story for her to make up, calling my aunt and uncle murderers of their own flesh! The least the girl deserves is a whipping.

"Which bracelet?"

Of course, my mother knows every bit of jewelry I own; it's her memory for detail that's allowed her to improve the family fortunes so much. "A, a gold chain, with trinkets on it," I say, with only a small hesitation. If Eliza got it in Paris, as she must have done, my mother won't ever have seen it on her. "I found it."

"Found it?" she repeats, her eyebrows soaring.

I'm sweating. "It was stoppered up in a bottle," I improvise; "it washed up on the levee."

"How peculiar."

"But it's mine," I repeat. "And Millie took it off my table while I was sleeping!"

Maman nods judiciously and turns away. "Do tidy yourself up before dinner, Aimée, won't you?"

We often have a guest to dinner; Creoles never refuse our hospitality to anyone who needs a meal or a bed for the night, unless he's a beggar. Today it's a slave trader who comes up and down the River Road several times a year; he has a long beard that gets things caught in it. Millie and two other house nègres carry in the dishes, lukewarm as always, since the kitchen is so far behind the house. Millie's face shows nothing; she can't have been punished yet. I avoid her eyes. I pick at the edges of my food; I've no appetite today, though I usually like poule d'eau—a duck that eats nothing but fish, so the Church allows it on Fridays. I listen to the trader and Maman discuss the cost of living, and sip my glass of claret. (Papa brings in ten thousand bottles a year from his estates at Château Bon-Air; our Famille is the greatest wine distributor in Louisiana.) The trader offers us our pick of the three males he has with him, fresh from the auction block at New Orleans, but Maman says with considerable pride that we breed all we need, and more.

After dinner I'm practicing piano in the salon—stumbling repeatedly over a tricky phrase of Beethoven's—when my mother comes in. "If you can't manage this piece, Aimée, perhaps you could try one of your Schubert's?" Very dry.

"Certainly, Maman."

"Here's your bracelet. A charming thing, if eccentric. Don't make a habit of fishing things out of the river, will you?"

"No, Maman." Gleeful, I fiddle with the catch, fitting it around my wrist.

"The girl claimed you'd given it to her as a present."

Guilt, like a lump of gristle in my throat.

"They always claim that, strangely enough," remarks my mother, walking away. "One would think they might come up with something more plausible."

The next day I'm in Tante Fanny's room, at my lessons. There was no sign of Millie this morning, and I had to dress myself; the girl must be sulking. I'm supposed to be improving my spelling of verbs in the subjunctive mode, but my stomach is a rat's nest, my dress is too tight, my head's fit to split. I gaze out the window to the yard, where the trader's saddling his mules. He has four nègres with him, their hands lashed to their saddles.

"Do sit down, child."

"Just a minute, Tante—"

"Aimée, come back here!"

But I'm thudding along the gallery, down the stairs. I trip over my hem, and catch the railing. I'm in the yard, and the sun is piercing my eyes. "Maman!"

She turns, frowning. "Where is your sunhat, Aimée?"

I ignore that. "But Millie—what's happening?"

"I suggest you use your powers of deduction."

I throw a desperate look at the girl, bundled up on the last mule, her mute face striped with tears. "Have you sold her?

She didn't do anything so very bad. I have the bracelet back safe. Maybe she only meant to borrow it."

My mother sighs. "I won't stand for thieving, or back-answers, and Millie has been guilty of both."

"But Pa Philippe, and her mother—you can't part her from them—"

Maman draws me aside, her arm like a cage around my back. "Aimée, I won't stoop to dispute my methods with an impudent and sentimental girl, especially in front of strangers. Go back to your lesson."

I open my mouth, to tell her that Millie didn't steal the bracelet, exactly; that she thought I had promised it to her. But that would call for too much explanation, and what if Maman found out that I've been interrogating the nègres about private family business? I shut my mouth again. I don't look at Millie; I can't bear it. The trader whistles to his mules to start walking. I go back into the house. My head's bursting from the sun; I have to keep my eyes squeezed shut.

"What is it, child?" asks Tante Fanny when I open the door. Her anger has turned to concern; it must be my face.

"I feel...weak."

"Sit down on this sofa, then. Shall I ring for a glass of wine?"

Next thing I know, I'm flat on my back, choking. I feel so sick. I push Tante Fanny's hand away. She stoppers her smelling salts. "My dear."

"What—"

"You fainted."

I feel oddly disappointed. I always thought it would be a luxuriant feeling—a surrendering of the spirit—but it turns out that fainting is just a sick sensation, and then you wake up.

"It's very natural," she says, with the ghost of a smile. "I believe you have become a woman today."

I stare down at myself, but my shape hasn't changed.

"Your petticoat's a little stained," she whispers, showing me the spots—some brown, some fresh scarlet—and suddenly I understand. "You should go to your room and ask Millie to show you what to do."

At the mention of Millie, I put my hands over my face.

"Where did you get that?" asks Tante Fanny, in a changed voice. She reaches out to touch the bracelet that's slipped out from beneath my sleeve. I flinch. "Aimée, where did you get that?"

"It was in a trunk, in the attic," I confess. "I know it was Eliza's. Can I ask you, how did she die?" My words astonish me as they spill out.

My aunt's face contorts. I think perhaps she's going to strike me. After a long minute, she says, "We killed her. Your uncle and I."

My God. So Millie told the truth, and in return I've had her sold, banished from the sight of every face she knows in the world.

"Your cousin died for our pride, for our greed." Tante Fanny puts her fingers around her throat. "She was perfect, but we couldn't see it, because of the mote in our eyes."

What is she talking about?

"You see, Aimée, when my darling daughter was about your age she developed some boutons."

Pimples? What can pimples have to do with anything?

My aunt's face is a mask of creases. "They weren't so very bad, but they were the only defect in such a lovely face, they stood out terribly. I was going to take her to the local root doctor for an ointment, but your papa happened to know a famous skin specialist in Paris. I think he was glad of the excuse for a trip to his native country. And we knew that nothing in Louisiana could compare to France. So your papa accompanied us—Eliza and myself and your Oncle Louis— on the long voyage, and he introduced us to this doctor. For eight days"—Tante Fanny's tone has taken on a biblical timbre—"the doctor gave the girl injections, and she bore it bravely. We waited for her face to become perfectly clear again—but instead she took a fever. We knew the doctor must have made some terrible mistake with his medicines. When Eliza died—" Here the voice cracks, and Tante Fanny lets out a sort of barking sob. "Your oncle wanted to kill the doctor; he drew his sword to run him through. But your papa, the peacemaker, persuaded us that it must have been the cholera or some other contagion. We tried to believe that; we each assured each other that we believed it. But when I looked at my lovely daughter in her coffin, at sixteen years old, I knew the truth as if God had spoken in my heart."

She's weeping so much now, her words are muffled. I wish I had a handkerchief for her.

"I knew that Eliza had died for a handful of pimples. Because in our vanity, our dreadful pride, we couldn't accept the least defect in our daughter. We were ungrateful, and she was taken from us, and all the years since, and all the years ahead allotted to me, will be expiation."

The bracelet seems to burn me. I've managed to undo the catch. I pull it off, the little gold charms tinkling.

Tante Fanny wipes her eyes with the back of her hand. "Throw that away. My curse on it, and on all glittering vanities," she says hoarsely. "Get rid of it, Aimée, and thank God you'll never be beautiful."

Her words are like a blow to the ribs. But a moment later, I'm glad she said it. It's better to know these things. Who'd want to spend a whole life hankering?

I go out of the room without a word. I can feel the blood welling, sticky on my thighs. But first I must do this. I fetch an old bottle from the kitchen, and a candle stub. I seal up the bracelet in its green translucent tomb, and go to the top of the levee, and throw it as far as I can into the Mississippi.

Vanitas

This imaginary reconstruction of the childhood of Aimée Locoul (1826–80) was inspired by a visit to the Laura Plantation (see www.lauraplantation.com) and Laura Locoul Gore's *Memories of the Old Plantation Home* and *A Creole Family Album* (2000).

When Aimée grew up, she helped her mother run the estate before marrying an impoverished French aristocrat, Charles Ivan Flavien de Lobel de Mahy; they had three children and divided the rest of their lives between Louisiana and France.

HOPEWELL, NEW JERSEY
1776

THE HUNT

He's fifteen, or thereabouts. He thought he would be home by Christmas. That was what they were told when they were given their red coats and shipped across the ocean to put down the rebs: that it wouldn't take more than a couple of months. But it's December already, and in New Jersey the snows are as dense as cake, and he thinks now that every soldier is told that: *home soon.* He wonders whether it's ever been true.

If the boy were in a German regiment, he could speak his own tongue at least. None of the English have even heard of Anhalt-Zerbst, let alone his village. He's never been to Hesse but his bunkmate says *you Hessians* anyway, or *you Bosch bastards.* Another points out that he's a foot or two short of a full one, so they settle on Half-Bosch.

Not soon, then, but how much longer? The redcoats took hard losses at Fort Mercer but cleaned out Fort Lee at the end of November. The rats are in retreat, and it's this regiment's job to squeeze them out of New Jersey. There's a line of the men of Hopewell outside the garrison every morning, wanting to sign allegiance papers—not that it proves much. Washington's reb army couldn't have held together

215

on its flight to Pennsylvania if this countryside weren't riddled with traitors, making muskets and shot for the rebs, supplying them with cloth for their backs and salt for their meat.

Some of this regiment have wives near their time, others say their wives are too pretty to leave alone; they all gripe about the endlessness of this campaign. The boy has only his mother. In the night, under the blanket, he thinks of his bed at home in his village in Anhalt-Zerbst and the way the fir tips tap against his window, and he weeps till he shakes. His bunkmate mutters, "Give that little worm of yours a rest."

Filthy talk is how they pass the time. In the freezing rains of December there's nothing to do but wait.

Then one day the skies clear. The land around Hopewell is as hard as a drum. "Good hunting weather," somebody says.

So the hunt is what they call it. The major isn't happy, but the captain only shakes his head and tells him, *The men must have a bit of fun.*

Houghton and Byrne and Williams and the boy start at a farmhouse on the edge of town. Muskets at the ready in case they flush out any rebs. The boy's stomach is tight, as on the verge of battle. Nobody answers the door until Byrne smashes the fanlight with his bayonet. Then they hear running feet, and the bar lifting. Byrne grabs the maid by her skirts but Williams says, "Hold hard, man. Where's your mistress, eh? Where's everybody hiding?"

She shakes her head, already sobbing.

The boy edges to one side.

"Where are you off to, Half-Bosch?"

"Search the house?"

"That's a lad," says Houghton, undoing his buttons one by one.

Upstairs the corridors are silent, except for the creakings his steps make. Far below him he can hear dull voices, then screaming that stops all at once. The boy peers into each room, taking his time. What will he do if he finds the ladies? *Yankee whores, reb whores.*

He goes down the back stairs. In the kitchen he eats a pickle from a jar; it's weaker than his mother's, it hardly tastes at all. He strokes the grain of an old settle, reads a sampler on the wall: *Her Price Is Above Rubies.*

Something clinks. He follows the small sound into the pantry, which seems to be empty, until he opens a small door and finds a girl crouching in the meat safe. Her hands fly to her ears.

"Monkey," he says under his breath.

"That's hardly civil!"

He points. "Hands on ears? Like the monkey in the picture."

She lowers her hands reluctantly. "Which picture?" Pale ears jut through her gleaming hair.

Like a pixie, he thinks. "Hear no bad."

"Oh, hear no evil, I see." She's crawling out and standing up, taller than he was expecting. A shiny apron, the kind that's just for show; a locket on a ribbon. "You're not English," she says accusingly.

"*Nein.*" He only slips when he's flustered.

"A mercenary!" Like something rotten in her mouth. The

boy must be looking blank, because she explains: "You serve for pay, for money."

"No money," he tells her. "I get my coat. Boots. Rations."

Which reminds him to examine the shelves. He finds a basket, grabs some jars, a cake in paper, the first dark bottle his hand falls on.

"Then, what brings you all the way to New Jersey?" she asks, close behind him.

"My prince sold me. To the redcoats." He crams three more bottles in on top of the cake.

"How could he sell you, when you're as white as me?" scoffs the girl. And then, "That's my aunt's best cherry brandy you're stealing."

"Requisitioning," he says, tripping over the English syllables.

"Half-Bosch!" The voice is Byrne's, faint but getting nearer.

The boy shoots out of the pantry with his basket. "Drink," he roars, "I found drink." He doesn't have time to look back.

He thinks about her, though. That night, in the barracks, when men are swapping dirty stories, and Williams and Houghton and Byrne are going on and on about the maid at the deserted farm—the boy pretends the brandy has put him to sleep. He squeezes his eyes shut and thinks of those pearly, sticking-out ears.

There's a rumor going round that Washington's reb army will melt away on New Year's Day, when the terms of service for most of his recruits come to an end. The boy tries to imagine being home for the spring planting.

The next day the hunt is on again. The redcoats trawl through Hopewell. There are scarlet ribbons on almost every door by now, but ribbon's cheap; it says loyalty without proving it. They knock on every door, and shout, "Bring out your females!" The boy stands guard outside the surgery while the others are inside with the doctor's wife and daughter. After half an hour, Williams sticks his head out the window to say, "Come on it, Half-Bosch, time we made a man of you."

He pulls a face. "Still sick from the damn brandy."

Williams grins and bangs the window shut so hard that an icicle falls like a spear.

"Let's go back to the farm," Houghton proposes that night. "I hate the thought of leaving a single maidenhead in the fucking State of New Jersey."

Williams laughs so hard he coughs.

In morning the fields crack like glass under the soldiers' boots. The boy doesn't want to be walking this way again, and he wants it more than anything. They get there in half an hour, and this time they go round to the back door: a stealth attack.

But the place is deserted; no sign of the maid even. The three Englishmen troop upstairs, and the boy heads for the pantry.

The girl's there, as he knew she'd be. She has some cheese for him; it's surprisingly strong. He finds himself telling her about the day he cut a purse from a gentleman's belt, back in Anhalt-Zerbst.

"I knew you were a thief."

He shrugs. "You're a reb."

"I am not!" Too loud for the narrow pantry. "I'm as loyal as you like. I never asked to come to this nest of traitors." Her hands shoot up to cup her ears.

Two feet away, he watches the tears brim along her lashes.

"My father was in the cavalry," she tells him. "So the rebs confiscated our farm in Pennsylvania, turned us out with only bedding and a plate each. Said my little brother had to stay to join their Patriot Army." Her voice skids. "Mamma sent us three elder girls off to relations, to be safe. She didn't know my aunt in Hopewell was a turncoat. And my cousins," she says, almost spitting, "they treat me like a rag to wipe their fingers on. They grudge me my dinner, won't lend me so much as a petticoat—"

His heart thumps dully in his chest. "Where are they hiding? Your aunt and cousins?"

Her pupils contract. "I don't know. A long way away," she says, without conviction.

"When did they leave?"

She shrugs. Her hands creep up through her hair.

He shocks himself by taking them in his. "Pretty ears. Don't cover them."

"You're making fun."

He shakes his head fervently. "Beautiful."

She finds him an apple. A knife to peel it. A slice for him, a slice for her. When he tries to kiss her, she pulls away, but slowly. Should he have asked first? Should he have insisted?

"Tell me where they are, these cousins who treat you so badly," he says, instead.

"It's just the elder girl, really."

"The men—the others in my company—they want women." He flushes, absurdly.

Her fingertips are pressing her ears to her head again, as if to stop them flying away.

"I must bring some women. You understand? Not you."

He thought she might weep, but she only looks into her lap. She says something, very low.

"What's that?"

"In the hayloft," she says, still whispering.

What he tells Williams and Houghton and Byrne, when he finds them upstairs filling their packs with silver plate, is that he heard voices in the barn. Williams whacks him on the back so hard it hurts. "We've got ourselves a good little hunting dog," he tells the others. "Bosch bloodhounds can't be beat."

In the barn, the boy is the last up the ladder. A child wails in the lap of a graying lady; a tall girl shrinks behind her. "Well, well, well," cries Houghton, rubbing his hands like some villain on a stage.

The aunt straightens up. "If it please you, sir—"

"Oh, you're going to please me well enough, madam, you're going to please every one of us."

Williams whoops at that.

"And anyone who puts up a fuss will get her ears cut off."

The boy hangs back. Mutters something about going for drink.

"Come, now, for the glory of the regiment," says Byrne, grabbing him by the elbow. "Fire away! Which d'you fancy—fresh meat or well aged?"

The older lady's eyes are as gray as his mother's. He wrenches himself out of Byrne's grasp, almost falls as he scrambles down the ladder.

The thing seems to go on for hours. He waits at the door of the barn, shivering in his thin red jacket.

That night he's the butt of the whole barracks. The captain puts his thumb on the boy's collarbone. "What's this I hear? Can't raise the regimental colors for the glory of King George?"

The boy doesn't know what the right answer is.

"Last chance, Half-Bosch," announces Houghton. "Tomorrow, the Major's off to Princeton for three days, so we're going to bring the tastiest fillies in Hopewell back to the garrison. If you don't produce some manner of female and show us you know how to put her through her paces..."

"The point is," says the captain, leaning in, breath fragrant with gin, "are you a girl or a man?" His grip shifts from collarbone to throat. "No two ways about it, Half-Bosch. Man or girl."

"I had one already," says the boy, pulling away in a fury of terror. "At the farm. I found her the first day. Much prettiest."

"Ooh, keeping the best for yourself, you rat!" Byrne cackles and smacks his shoulder. "Well, bring her back tomorrow and show us what you're made of."

What he's made of? It's not a phrase the boy has heard before; it makes him think of the gingerbread boy, who ran and ran until the fox snapped him up.

He wakes before dawn and lies like a corpse. He can't

feel his feet. He finds himself thinking of his mother's softly creased hands, setting down a bowl of borscht before him. He shoves the memory away. His mother would not know him. He sees as clear as lightning that he will never go home.

By noon he's kneeling beside the girl in the pantry, holding on to her hands. He tries not to hear the shouting in the distance.

"They hate me," she says again.

"How do they know it was—"

"They don't, they hated me before. But now they hate me because I wasn't in the hayloft. My aunt's demented." Her pupils are huge and dark. "The little one's not twelve. I never thought—"

"I wasn't there," he whispers, eyes down. *Yankee whores, rebel whores.*

"She's been bleeding all night."

The distant voices are rising. Clarity seizes him. "You come with me now," he says, jerking his head in the direction of the fields.

"Run away with you? Are you mad? I couldn't dream of it," she says, but her face is bright.

She's misunderstood him, but he sees his chance; he leans in and kisses her. It's not what he was expecting; lighter, more feathery. "You're my girl," he says then in a deep voice.

"I barely know you," she says.

She's smiling so widely that he knows he's won, and something sinks in his chest. "I won't go without you," he says.

"But my aunt, my—Where are you going?"

He hesitates. "Who knows?"

"They'll catch you. Won't they?"

He manages a shrug. He gets to his feet, not letting go of her hand.

"Let me run upstairs and pack my trunk..."

The boy shakes his head, alarmed at the thought of having to carry such a thing. "No time, little monkey. Just your coat."

Outside, panting from the hurry, she's daunted by the icy fields. "Don't you have anything for me to ride?"

"I'll lift you over the puddles," he offers.

The girl laughs. "I can jump them."

And for a moment, as they set off across the meadow hand in hand like children, he lets himself believe that they are running away. That he is man enough to be a deserter. That there's anywhere he could take this girl without being tracked down and sent back to Hopewell in chains and hanged in front of his company. That he could bring her all the way home with him to taste his mother's borscht.

But all the while he knows how it's going to be. He will lead her into the barracks that must be already filling up with other girls, girls with torn sleeves and bloody noses and scalps, reb girls and loyal, girls whose eyes will tell this girl all she needs to know. When the captain claps and orders Half-Bosch to fire away, this girl will start to scream, and the boy will reach down with frozen fingers and undo his buttons one by one.

The Hunt

Sharon Block's *Rape and Sexual Power in Early America* (2006) documents the moment in 1776 when British and German troops in New Jersey and Staten Island started systematically attacking the female population. A cavalry commander named Lord Rawdon quipped, "The fair nymphs of this isle are in wonderful tribulation, a girl cannot step into the bushes to pluck a rose without running the most imminent risk of being ravished." Sixteen girls from Hopewell were held for days on end in a garrison; the rest is my invention.

NEW YORK CITY
1901

DADDY'S GIRL

I just now came up from seeing Daddy.

I never walked in here without knocking before. His study is real cold; the back of his big chair is smooth like an icicle. I know every object in this room, but it is as if I have never stepped across the threshold before.

The newspaper folded on the desk says January 18, 1901. I still can't get used to it, this century I mean. It sounds most improbable.

Doctor Gallagher said he would have to show me if I couldn't take his word for it. But I've never seen Daddy without his necktie, even. I guess I always thought he was a modest kind of man. So when it came to it, today, I just couldn't bear to lift the sheet that went up to his chin.

Daddy's face looked kind of peeved, like when Momma was alive and dinner went on too long and I could tell he wanted to stroll down to the saloon on Seventh and smoke a great black cigar.

He looked the same last Saturday, the last time I saw him—only he seemed clammy, then, somehow. Was it the pain? It strikes me now, he must have known; he must have felt it coming. Nobody ever could pull the wool over Daddy's eyes. He called me in—he was sitting right here in this chair—and he told me to go stay with my friends in Brooklyn for a week. No reason given, no questions to be asked. No, I wasn't to call home on the telephone; he didn't want to be disturbed. "Get on, girl." I thought it must of had something to do with politics.

I reckon we ought to bury him right away. Before the reporters burst in and get a look at him.

Why couldn't Doctor Gallagher have kept his big mouth shut and let a man rest in peace? I don't see that the public's got a right to know. There was a fellow from the *New York Times* on the stairs five minutes ago, hollering though the keyhole. "Miss Hall, Miss Hall. Could you tell? How long have you known? Are you in the dimes now, Miss Hall? Is it true you've netted a cool million?"

All today I have kept a good hold on myself, because I am known to my friends as the sort of girl you can rely on, but now it is all starting to shake loose. My mind runs round in little circles. I feel banished from my old life.

My name is Miss Imelda Hall, known as Minnie. I am twenty-two years of age. I help—used to help—my daddy, Mr. Murray Hall, run an employment agency at 145 Sixth Avenue. My daddy was an important man in New York, a pillar of the Democratic Party.

All in all, I am glad I didn't lift the sheet. There are some things you shouldn't look at, because what are you supposed to do afterwards? Like that thing I saw once in a trash can behind the market, I believe it was a baby.

Oh, my good Jesus.

If Daddy was here now, he'd give Bridget a smack around the head for letting the fire go out.

He left his hat on his desk. Inside it's black with grease.

Why, what a fool I was, we all were. Daddy's friends used to complain that all the years they were going bald as taters, he never lost a hair off his head. And another thing, his face is always smooth, as if he's come up directly from the barber's, even when I know for a fact he's only just got out of bed.

I should have wondered about that, shouldn't I? But a girl's not inclined to set to wondering, when it's her own daddy and he doesn't care for being stared at. And he never seemed like anything but your regular poker-playing whiskey-drinking good fellow. Not exactly handsome, but a real charmer with the ladies.

It turns my stomach.

How could Momma? How could she? Unless she didn't know. Could that be true? Could you be married to someone without the slightest idea who they were? And what about all his other girls, don't tell me none of them knew. I can't decide who's the real deviant.

I am sitting here in Daddy's study at Daddy's desk in Daddy's big leather chair, and any minute now he is going to walk in here and catch me.

I know what he would rather I did. "Put a match to the whole damn lot," he'd say; "no use rooting around in a dead man's papers."

But the thing is, Daddy, I'm a little curious. And this is not your private study anymore. You're not really going to come across the landing and find me poking about, are you? I can do what I please now.

The thing is, quite above and beyond the thing itself, this changes everything. For instance, if Daddy's not my daddy, who is? I just can't see a fine upstanding woman like Momma carrying on with another... with a man. Did he tell her, "Go right ahead, Cecilia, don't mind me"? I just cannot see Daddy putting up with that kind of malarkey.

I'm counting on him to have left something, some kind of clue. Surely it would be here if it was anywhere, wedged in one of these bursting drawers or pigeonholes, slipped in between these old campaign handbills and Democratic Party meeting notices and postal cards to "good old Murray Hall."

Something you never got around to mentioning, something you always wanted to say. You and Momma did plan to tell me, didn't you? I expect you just didn't quite know how to broach it. Surely you didn't reckon to let me go my whole life through, not knowing who in the heck I am?

This must be it. I knew it would be here. So simple, a folded paper with "Minnie" on the outside: I can hardly bear to open it.

"Gone to hustings, home late, don't wait dinner."

Damn him. His notes were never more than ten words long.

This desk is full of the junk of a whole lifetime. My stomach is growling now. I'm dizzy, adrift, lost in a sea of old papers. But what I'm looking for must be in here somewhere.

He always said I had Momma's eyes and his nose. The senator used to say, "Isn't she the dead spit of her daddy?"

I must have been adopted.

Now I am making a right mess and papers are falling on the rug but I don't care. It has got to be written down, surely. Where I was born, how they got me. There must be a letter or a certificate or a photograph, even. Something with my name on.

Could be my name is not my name, of course. It could be staring me blue in the face and I'd never recognize it. Could be I had another name before they adopted me and turned me into Miss Imelda (Minnie) Hall. Maybe I am not an Imelda but a Priscilla or an Agnes. And of course I am not a Hall either. God knows what I am. A stray, a foreigner? Come to think of it, I've got no proof I'm twenty-two years old. Could be it's all lies.

I am not rightly anyone or anything now. Just like a bit of orange peel floating down the gutter.

It makes me shake to think of it. Not about my name so much as about Daddy. When I think of him now, I could just rip him to pieces.

I am quite an independent person. My friends and I go all over the city on the subway trains. I have been up the New York World Building, twenty-two stories high, and seen a moving picture at Koster and Bial's. (It was a man sneezing, that's all, but still.) Yet Daddy has always been able to cut me down to size and make me feel like a little idiot girl. When the cycle craze started and I longed for a machine of my own, he said I was too young, and even when I turned twenty-one and asked again, he said surely I wasn't so immodest as to want to pedal around town in bloomers. Then the other day I came down all ready for a party and Daddy made a very cutting remark about the neck of my bodice. I told him it was all the rage, but he said I might as well serve up my bosoms on a plate for the fellows. He made me go right upstairs and change my whole ensemble and I was late for the party. And to think that all this time, all these years—well, there's no other way to put it, but Daddy had bosoms himself.

What kind of monster plays a trick that lasts a lifetime? What kind of woman decides to be a man?

These cards are so old they've gone yellow. "Best of wishes from all the boys to good old Murray Hall." "With the compliments of State Senator Barney Martin to his old friend Murray Hall." "Merry Christmas, dear Murray, from all your pals on the Committee."

I never could stay awake when Daddy talked Tammany Hall. Who'd promised his vote in which ward, and which man could be trusted, and which other fellow would slit your throat as soon as look at you. How Daddy'd started out as a nobody fresh off the boat and now he was a professional bondsman, but best of all, he was rich in friends, and what else could a man rely on in this world?

There was that one time Daddy got wild at Skelly's on Tenth Avenue and whipped a policeman in the street, ended up in the station house. But his buddies squared it in the right quarters, and he was home for breakfast. Momma had been worried near out of her mind. But the Democrats can fix anything in New York. Sometimes it takes a bribe or a riot or maybe even a body in the river, I've heard, but the job gets done. You keep on the right side of the Tammany Hall men, Daddy used to say, you wear a permanent smile.

I wonder what they would say if they could see him now. If they lifted the sheet, as I cannot bear to do. I don't need to lift it; after all, I know what I'd see. Like looking in some funhouse mirror.

When I went over to draw the curtains just now, I could hear those jackal reporters down below, shouting up at me. "Miss Hall, Miss Hall." But I will not talk to them. They put words in a person's mouth.

Yes! Here it is in my hand: "The Last Will and Testament."

It doesn't take long to read.

Well, I guess I needn't worry about anyone marrying me for my money. Oh, Daddy. Was *any* of it true?

It's not that I'm not grateful for the two hundred dollars, but where's all the rest gone? What kind of deals did those friends of yours do? And I see that out of that sum I'm supposed to "cause to be erected a suitable headstone over the grave of Cecilia, the deceased wife of the testator." That is a sweet thought, Daddy, but what would a "suitable headstone" for Momma say? *I Married a Woman, Lord Forgive Me?*

Momma will just have to move on over and make room; I surely can't afford two headstones if I'm to feed myself this winter. I bet she knew. She was a sweet-looking woman, was Momma, even if she was twice Daddy's size. Now there is a queer thought: I don't expect a layperson can spot the difference between a man and a woman after a few years in the grave, when you get down to the plain bones.

Daddy was never seen around the Lower West Side without some class of female on his arm. Younger than me, sometimes; even the maids who came to our office looking for a job. He just couldn't keep his hands off the opposite...I mean, girls. It saddened Momma so, she stopped speaking to Daddy years before she died.

But I've got to try to be merciful, I suppose. There's nobody else left to forgive him. I guess he had simply got to be a man's man, and a ladies' man, and every kind of man, so no one would suspect he was no such thing. Doing his best to fit in, play the game, when in Rome, that sort of thing. I bet he was sick when he tasted his first cigar, but he kept right on. And he got so he could drink his weight in beer and stand up under it too. As if he'd found a book on being a man and was set on following it page by page.

It strikes me now that I do not even know where Daddy came from. He sometimes used to talk about making the crossing, but he never said from where, exactly. Daddy didn't care to be interrupted with questions when he was telling a story. His tales made the crossing sound such a hoot: all the farmers down in steerage green as grass, and the fiddler carrying on regardless. He had an accent, but not like anyone else's I've known. Could it have been Ireland he started out from? Or Scotland?

I wonder now if it was an adventure, at first, or an escape? Was he hiding from somebody, the first time he put on a cap and a pair of trousers, or did he just like the feel of them? Could he have guessed it would be for always?

Daddy never said much about his life from before he

crossed the ocean. Whatever I asked him, he claimed he couldn't remember. He liked to say that if you looked back you'd turn to salt. What a curious phrase, "turn to salt." Did he mean tears? He once said there was nothing set his teeth on edge more than an emigrant sniveling for home.

He doesn't have a name now either, no more than me. I wonder what he was born. Mary Hall? Jane Hall? Or no kind of Hall at all?

I almost set to laughing when I think of calling Daddy by a girl's name, and him in no position to stop me. Oh Lord, I could cry to think of him as a Nancy or Eliza.

I don't even know how old he was when he arrived. I see him at the rail of the ship, heading past the Statue of Liberty, but his face is blank. What is he wearing? I wish I could be there, a foot away, looking at the skyline. Just for a moment. Just to ask why it's so bad to be a woman.

I guess I could have been a better daughter. I used to get uppity with him when he would forget his key and haul on the bell when he crashed in at two in the morning, especially after Momma died. Daddy used to say I'd inherited his temper and Momma's sulks together, but now it turns out my faults are all my own.

No wonder he drank. Doctor Gallagher says it was a cancer in the left breast. He says Daddy must have been sick for years and years and never said a word; the cancer had worked right through to the heart. It sounds like woodworm, I can't help thinking, or like when the mice get into the cheese. What a ninny I was; I thought all those books on medicine Daddy collected were some sort of hobby. I saw him take a spoonful from a bottle once but he said it was cod-liver oil. Five years of being eaten away, for fear of being found out.

The papers are all in one big heap now, and I'm so cold I had best go down to the kitchen. There's nothing left to read. Only one last drawer that comes unstuck with a shudder, and there's nothing in it but a bit of card at the back.

An old brown photograph: a girl with too many ringlets. One of his hussies from the early days? That goes on the top of the pile, facedown; I'll toss the lot in the range after supper.

Unless.

It couldn't be.

Daddy?

I turn the picture up, and all of a sudden it changes; I see past the ringlets, into the face. It looks like Daddy dressed up as a girl, for a game. Eyebrows drawn together; a faint smile.

I *have* got his nose.

Well, he looked better in trousers. But I will tuck the picture into my pocket. I did not know before today that you can hate and despise a person and still love him on the other side of all that.

He is still my daddy. Even if he is dead. And a woman.

Doctor Gallagher says "she," now, when he remembers, and so do the reporters. But I won't, not ever. Daddy wouldn't like it.

Daddy's Girl

According to the death certificate, Murray Hall died on January 16, 1901, and was born around 1831—so lived to be nearly seventy. But nothing about Hall is certain. Born perhaps Mary Anderson, or Mary or Elizabeth Hall, Murray Hall was said to have come from Ireland, Scotland, or New York's Lower West Side. Hall's first wife died, or disappeared; the second marriage ended in estrangement after about seven, or perhaps twenty, years. This jumble of facts and speculations comes from the *New York Times* (January 18 and 19 and March 20, 1901), the *New York Tribune* (January 18, 20, and 29 and March 20, 1901), *Munzey's Magazine* (1901, including pictures), and *The Weekly Scotsman* (February 9, 1901).

Minnie (Imelda) Hall was only twenty-two when her famous father was posthumously exposed as female. One of the few things we know about Minnie is that she refused to talk to reporters. At the inquest she was prompted to refer to her father as "she," but retorted, "I will never say she."

NEWMARKET, ONTARIO

1967

WHAT REMAINS

She hasn't asked for me in two months. I check with her nurses, though it's a little humiliating. "Has Miss Loring by any chance asked for me?" I say. Lightly, as if it doesn't matter either way.

That's what they call her: Miss Loring, or sometimes Frances. She's not Queenie to anyone but me.

I wheeled myself into her room today. She was lying there like a beached whale ready for the ax. "Queenie," I said, "it's me. It's Florence." Which sounded absurd, as I've never had to tell her who I am before, she always knew. What a pass we've come to, if I need to introduce myself! Like that line in the Bible: *The people who walk in darkness.* Brains rot like fruit in the end. I don't pity her for going senile. It's worse being a witness.

I try to keep a grip on the numbers, myself. The nurses start to worry if you get the numbers wrong. It's 1967 and I'm eighty-five years old. I should by rights be dead. Queenie's not even eighty. I ought to have gone first. It shouldn't be like this.

I always thought it would be all right so long as we ended

up in the same place. She collapsed just before our final exhibition, and I fell sick a week later, and when we were both moved to this Home just north of Toronto, I thought, Well, at least we'll be together. No need to fuss with cooking or shovel our own snow anymore; we'll get to talk all day if we want.

But there's more than one kind of distance that can come between people. This is our third year here. Her door says Miss F. Loring, mine says Miss F. Wyle, and they might as well be a thousand miles apart, instead of a fifty-foot corridor. Since Queenie's last attack, her eyes barely move when I wheel into her room, and she doesn't seem to recognize my name.

What's important, I suppose, is for me to keep remembering. What matters is to hold on to what's left.

Each one must go alone down the dark valley.

I wrote that poem a long time ago, before I knew what I was talking about.

My father used to say man was the only creature capable of sleeping on his back, so that was how we should sleep. To mark the difference, you see; to show that we were a Higher Form. I did try; I started every night flat on my back, but it hurt my bones and I couldn't breathe. My father would come to wake me in the morning and find me curled up on my side and shake me awake. "Florence," he'd roar, "you look like an animal!"

When I was six I found a rooster with a broken leg. I fixed him just fine, mostly because my father said I'd never manage it. It was animals that turned me toward art. I saw a bird, and then a picture of a bird, and it all came together. If I couldn't be a bird, then at least I could make one. Once a cat of ours died, and I asked if God had taken her to heaven, and my father said there was no room for animals in heaven. That's the day I stopped believing in God. Rosa Bonheur, the French sculptor, believed in metempsychosis, which means that human souls migrate into either human or animal forms. She lived with her friend and a whole ark of animals and painted them. I suppose it seemed to her that we're all just creatures in the end.

Mind you, I'd shoot a dog if it got as crazy as Queenie.

Sixty years this month since we met in that Clay Modeling class in Chicago. She was big and I was small. She was beautiful and I was not. Her family adored her and mine didn't care for me. She grew up in Geneva, Switzerland; I came from Waverly, Illinois. She thought she liked men and I thought I hated them. She had faith in politics and I wrote poems about trees. She worked in spurts; I did a little every day. All we had in common was a taste for clay.

Today her hands lie on the sheet like withered bananas. I remember a time when they were swift and sure and tireless. Like the Skeena River in full flood, that time I went to the Indian village to model the old totem poles. When was that? Back in the twenties sometime? Damn it. Gone.

That's us these days, a couple of old totem poles. Tilting at mad angles, silvery as ash, fading into the forest.

At the Art Institute in Chicago, the master used to pinch all us girls on the bottom. He called it the *droit de maître*. Queenie didn't much mind. I slapped his hand away and called him a damn fool. Later he spread a rumor we were a couple of Sapphists.

There was another thing Queenie used to say: *You can't go through life worrying about what people think of you.*

Some days she's got more of a grip than others. She still doesn't ask for me, but when I go into her room she sometimes seems to know who I am.

I tell her uplifting stories. "Remember Adelaide Johnson, Queenie?"

A flicker of the eyes.

"She was barely twenty when she fell down that elevator shaft in the Chicago Music Hall. Did it stop her?"

"Hell, no," says Queenie feebly.

I laugh out loud. "That's right. She won fifteen thousand dollars in damages and went off to study her art in Europe!"

But Queenie's face is blank, like a block of marble that's never been touched by the chisel.

I will not feed my soul with sorrow, that was her favorite line in all my poems.

Some dates are so clear in my head it's as if they're chiseled there. We came to Toronto in 1913. Canada was a young country; there seemed infinite room. But we only really got established after the Great War. The towns needed so many memorials, they had to stoop to hiring women! Queenie used to say that her career was built on dead boys.

Sculptors, we called ourselves from the start. The word "sculptress" sets my teeth on edge. Work like ours called for sensible clothes. We took to trousers, as early as the twenties, plus men's shoes and baggy jackets.

I'm not allowed to wear my old gray flannels here. I suspect they've been thrown in the trash. Well, they were a little decrepit, I admit. Instead, the nurses give me housecoats to put on, pink or orange: hideous. "Blue was my color, Queenie, do you remember?" I usually wore a touch of pale blue.

Queenie was always the more bohemian dresser. At our studio parties she'd appear in purple velvet with a gold fringe, or a green satin cape. I told her once she looked like something out of the comic strips—the Caped Crusader, or the Emerald Evil—and she wasn't too pleased. There was always a trail of ash across her front because she was too busy talking to remember the ashtray.

They keep her clean and tidy here; that's another reason she doesn't look like herself. And you can't get hold of a cigarette for love nor money.

I am lost in this forest of days. I can't remember when I wrote that. I go through a sort of checklist of names in my head, in case I'm forgetting anything. Our dogs were Samson and Delilah. (Delilah tore our neighbor's fur coat, but it served her right for wearing such a thing.) We had two motor cars, first Susie, then Osgoode. (Queenie always drove, and never got any better at it; I read the maps.) Some of our sculptures were—are, I mean—*Dream Within a Dream, Women War Workers, Torso, Girl with Fish, The Goal Keeper, Negro Woman, The Rites of Spring, Derelicts, Eskimo Mother and Child, The Miner, Sea and Shore, The Key.* There were others, I know there were others, but I can't recall their names just now. Some are sold, some are scattered, the rest are under dust sheets in our cold locked-up studio in Toronto that was a derelict church until we moved in. I don't have any of them here, but I can see them more clearly than my own mother's face.

The thing about sculpture is, it's always a risk. It costs money to model it, cast it, carve it, even transport it. Clay's bad enough; bronze is terrible; marble's ruinous.

All this week Queenie's been yapping away in her head to old friends, dead or alive or who knows. Sometimes if I listen closely I can pick up hints of who it is. Yesterday I could tell it was A. Y. Jackson, because she was thanking him for taking us out to dinner the day he sold his first picture. He and she seemed to be having a grand old time.

She always did like parties better than I. We had forty-eight artists for Christmas one year, as well as three beggars from the neighborhood. Six turkeys got eaten down to the bone. In the evening there was chamber music, and I drank too much wine and was persuaded to show them all how to do an Illinois hog call.

"Remember Liz Prophet, Queenie?"

"Mm," she says, ambiguously.

"That awful gallery in Rhode Island, they said they had nothing against showing a black girl's sculptures so long as she promised not to come to the opening. Barbarians! Do you remember what she did, Queenie?"

Silence.

I fill in with barely a pause. "Ran away to gay Paree."

"That's right," whispers Queenie.

"That's right," I repeat. "Lived on tea and marmalade."

"Stole food from dogs."

This detail cheers me immensely. Her memory's still in there, like the shape locked inside the marble. "That's right, my dear, Liz Prophet had to steal food from Parisian dogs. What was it you used to say to me in our bad winters? *No one's got a right to call herself an artist until she's starved a little!*"

Her eyes have gone unfocused, milky blue.

She still keeps that photograph on her bedside table, the one of Charlie Mulligan, who taught her marble cutting back in the 1900s. "Isn't he a fine fellow?" she's taken to asking the nurses, sometimes four times a day. I bet she doesn't remember his name either.

"Was he your young man, Miss Loring?" one of them said this morning, to humor her.

"That's right."

"Was he the love of your life?"

"That's right, that's right," Queenie repeats in a whisper, like a child. "The love of my life."

She doesn't mean Charlie Mulligan, by the way. That wild German she nearly married back in 1914, he's the one she used to call the love of her life. Not that I know what that means. Which life is she talking about when she says stupid things like that? As far as I know, the life she had was the one she spent with me.

> *I will not feed my soul with sorrow,*
> *Not while dark trees march in naked majesty.*

When I wrote that, ten years ago, we still had the farm: a hundred and fifty acres of wild quince and poison ivy by the

Rouge River. These days I have a room with a small window facing onto the parking lot. I haven't seen a tree in a while.

Queenie doesn't know anyone today. She's got butter on her double chin.

A journalist once asked her, "Miss Loring, do you specialize in memorial sculpture because of a special sympathy for the dear departed?"

I had to cut in; I couldn't resist. "No," I said, "it's because she likes climbing ladders."

It was true. She's always liked to work on a grand scale. She's built on a grand scale too.

The local children used to call us the Clay Ladies. That was because we showed them how to make things out of clay, of course, but the phrase fitted us too, more and more as the decades went by. These days we look like works in progress, there's no point pretending otherwise. Queenie's a vast model for a monument—all two hundred pounds of her clay slapped onto a gigantic wire armature—and as for me, I'm some skinny leftover. Maybe I'm a Giacometti and she's a Henry Moore! Not that I'm a fan of the so-called moderns; most of them couldn't draw a human body if they tried, and as for beauty, I doubt they could even spell it. Boring holes in things!—that's not sculpture, that's vandalism.

To think she and I used to be something. A unit; a name. The Loring-Wyles.

I'm not saying it was all fun and games. We had a couple of bad years. We sometimes considered suicide, only half joking. But we didn't think we should depart alone; we wanted to take at least a dozen enemies with us. On dark February evenings in the studio we amused ourselves by drawing up a list.

But if there's no heaven, what remains?

All this week Queenie's been having delusions. She sits up in bed, the sheets draped around her like snow on the Niagara Escarpment. She shakes her fists over her head and pants with effort. The nurses say if she doesn't calm down she's going to bring on another attack.

Finally today I figured out what she's doing. She thinks she's carving her lion, all over again.

"Why a lion?" I asked her, nearly thirty years ago.

She laughed. "Isn't it obvious, Florence? A snarling, defiant lion; rising from a crouch, ready for a fight."

Well, this was 1940.

It was to be a huge, stylized sort of lion, guarding the entrance to the new Queen Elizabeth Way near Toronto, to commemorate the visit of the king and queen. I wouldn't have thought it was possible to do anything new with a lion, but Queenie's design was a wonder: the beast's face and ruff and whole muscled body were made up of great smooth arcs of stone.

It was just about the most grueling project Queenie ever dragged us into, and that's saying something. I say "we," but I was only doing a bas-relief of Their Majesties on the back of the column. Queenie's lion had to be carved on site, emerging from the column, as it were. She planned to use Indiana limestone—lovely, flawless stuff—but no, word came down that for patriotic reasons it had to be Queenston limestone, which was twice as hard and pocked with holes. That was bad enough, but hiring a stonecutter was the worst. The top three men on our list were struck off by government order as "enemy aliens," even though the German had been reared in Canada and the Italians were the best in the trade. Instead, Queenie had to put up with a true-blue Englishman whose work she'd never trusted.

He couldn't take orders from a woman, that was his problem, and he wasn't the only one, let me tell you. We had to scour the country to find a cutting machine for the fellow, and he still didn't get started till August of that year. When we drove down in November to check his progress, the rough outlines of the lion had only half-emerged from the column. "The fellow hasn't even started on the hind quarters," muttered Queenie.

I thought the neck looked a little odd. Queenie asked him about it. "Oh, yes, actually, Miss Loring," said the fellow, avoiding her eyes, "I changed the line a little, to make it lie better."

The cheek of the man! I didn't blame her for firing him on the spot, even with all the horrors that followed.

Queenie couldn't find another qualified cutter in Canada. She consulted the union, who told her that only their members were permitted to cut stone for sculpture. She told the union to go to hell, she'd finish it herself.

Neither of us had ever used a cutting machine. The December winds howled in off the lake. I remember craning up at Queenie on the scaffold, which we'd swathed in tarpaulins as a feeble shelter. She was fifty-two that year, and already a huge woman. Her hands were swollen with arthritis.

"Queenie!"

"Don't you fret, Florence," she shouted down.

"It's not worth it," I bawled. "Give it up!"

She pretended not to hear. I could tell, from the way she handled the machine, that she was in pain. The planks of the scaffold buckled under her weight. Specks of snow fell on her head.

I cursed her, but the wind ate up my words. "What if you fall?" I screeched.

She peered over the tarpaulin, her face drawn but hilarious. "I'll probably bounce!"

She didn't fall. Next day she abandoned the machine and picked up her biggest chisel and hammer. If I'd been a praying sort of woman, I'd have prayed then. As it was, I stood and shivered and watched, week after week. I remember wondering what would happen to us all if Hitler won the war.

The snow held off just long enough. The lion crawled from his block, metamorphosing like something out of Ovid. By the time Queenie dropped her tools, her hands were like claws but the lion was magnificent.

On his pedestal, in deep-cut letters, it said something about "the Empire's darkest hour" and this work having been done "in full confidence of victory and a lasting peace." I remember it because it was on the day of the highway's official opening, as we stood below the lion with the lake wind lashing our scarves against our numb faces, that it occurred to me that I was a Canadian. Not that in thirty years I'd ever got around to filling in the forms; on paper I was—as I am still—a U.S. citizen. But sometimes things about you change without you noticing.

So that's how the story ended. Only for Queenie, I see now, it's not over. It's 1967 but she can't be convinced her war work is done. She still straddles the scaffolding, high above Lake Ontario. Her hands grip huge imaginary tools. "Just another quarter inch," she mumbles hoarsely.

"Lie down, now," I tell her. "Nurse says it's time for your sponge bath."

"In a minute," she says, austere. Her arm moves as if to hammer the air, and she speaks to me as if I'm a stranger. "I don't think you appreciate the urgency of my work."

"Of course I do," I murmur.

Then her head turns, and her blue eyes bore into mine, and her voice rises. "It may have escaped your attention," she roars, "but there's a war going on!"

"But, Queenie," I say for the hundredth time, "your lion's finished."

She gives me a weary look, as if she sees through all my wiles.

"Everyone loves him! They say he's the finest monumental sculpture in Canada." Well, that's not quite a lie; some people did say that, once.

She shakes her head. "I still need to do his ears. And his back paws, and his tail."

"No, he's all done. I'll prove it," I say rashly. And then it occurs to me that I can.

I've struck a deal with the Home's handyman. But the head nurse says she'll have to speak to the authorities. "On

the Queen Elizabeth Way, Miss Wyle?" she repeats, uncon-
vinced.

"Just at the entrance."

"A lion?"

"You must have seen it," I tell her. "You couldn't miss it
if you've ever driven down to Niagara."

And then it occurs to me that she thinks I'm the one who's
gone gaga. Delusions of lions. "It's a stone lion," I clarify
coldly. "You may not know that Miss Loring and I are sculptors. Our work is to be found in many cities and galleries
across Canada."

"Yes," she says, as if placating me.

"Besides," I snap, "as far as I am aware, we are voluntary
residents here. If we choose to be taken on a drive by a kind
young man on his afternoon off, I can't see that you have any
right to object."

She butts in. "Miss Loring isn't strong—"

"My friend is well enough to sit in a motor car. It's her
mind that's troubled. And what I propose to do will set her
mind at rest."

I sound more sure than I am.

The air smells clean. The May sunshine dazzles me. I cover
my eyes.

A Bug, the young handyman calls it. Looks like a Henry
Moore car to me; all bulges and holes. He lifts me out of my
wheelchair and puts me in first, then I help to tug Queenie in
through the other door. Occasionally she laughs. It takes us a
quarter of an hour. I can tell the boy's surprised at my strength.
My legs may be kaput but my skinny arms are still a sculptor's.

"Are you comfortable, Miss Loring?"

No answer from Queenie, who's examining one of her knees as if she's never seen it before.

The boy gives me a doubtful glance.

"Yes, yes, she's fine, let's be off," I tell him. So he wheels our chairs back into the Home, then starts up the engine.

Toronto is a blur of sunlight and glass high rises. I glance idly into shop windows—bikinis, Muskoka chairs, sunflowers—not letting myself wonder if this is the last time I'll ever see the city.

We're at the Queen Elizabeth Way in less than an hour. The lake glitters like tinsel. Our driver looks over his shoulder. "Where do you want me to stop, Miss Wyle?"

"Just by the entrance."

"Oh. Only, I don't think it's legal. I mean, everyone else is going pretty fast."

"Let them," I say, autocratic. "Park on the verge."

"Couldn't I just slow down a bit as we go past this statue of yours?"

"No, you could not. Pull over."

He wheels onto the shoulder and we come to a shuddering stop. "It's dangerous," he remarks. "What if the cops come by?"

"Tell them you've got two octogenarians having heart attacks in the back of your car."

That shuts him up. He turns off the engine.

I roll down my window jerkily and lean out, squinting into the sun. "Look, Queenie, your lion!"

She keeps on staring into her lap. The boy sits with his arms folded, as if embarrassed by us.

I lean over her bulk and tug at the handle till the dirty glass slides down. "Go on," I say eagerly. "Put your head out and have a look. He's finished. He's splendid."

Finally she seems to hear me. She leans her head to one side, lolling out the window. Dust blows in her face as a chain of cars rushes by. I hang out the window on my side and stare at the stone beast, as good as new if a little darker. Nearly thirty years, and not a mark on him. He could stand there forever. There, I want to tell Queenie, that's what remains of us.

I reach over to take her hand. But she has her head down again; she seems to be examining an egg stain on her lapel. A dreadful thought occurs to me. I let go of her hand and wave my fingers in front of her face. She doesn't flinch.

"Queenie?"

She looks in my direction. Her eyes are calm and milky. She can't see a thing.

I should have guessed. I should have remembered her eyes were getting worse; I would have, if I'd half a brain left myself.

"What do you think of your lion now?" I ask her softly, just to be sure.

She says nothing for a minute, and then, "Lion?"

I don't answer her. After a minute I lean over to roll up her window. Then I tell the boy he can take us back to the Home now.

An enormous tiredness settles on me. I lay my head on the seat back at a peculiar angle. I shut my eyes to escape from the sunlight. *Each one must go alone down the dark valley.* I keep hold of Queenie's hand, but only because I can't think of anything else to do.

"Blue," she murmurs, half an hour later at a traffic light, and I don't know what she means: the lake? the sky? or just what she remembers of the color that used to go by that name?

"That's right," I say, "blue."

What Remains

Frances "Queenie" Loring (1887–1968) and Florence Wyle (1881–1968) decided to move from the United States to Canada for the sake of their careers as sculptors; they spent almost sixty years together in Toronto. This story draws on Rebecca Sisler's anecdotal life *The Girls* (1972), and some of Florence Wyle's published poems, but more recently the "Loring-Wyles" have been granted the thorough biography they deserve, Elspeth Cameron's *And Beauty Answers: The Life of Frances Loring and Florence Wyle* (2007). Loring's lion, part of the *Queen Elizabeth Monument,* was moved in 1975 to Sir Casimir Gzowski Park on Lakeshore Boulevard West, Toronto.

After passing a few years with Loring at a nursing home in Newmarket, Ontario, Wyle too developed dementia, and they died within three weeks of each other in 1968.

AFTERWORD

I don't know where I am. I peer out the little window at the flat landscape hurtling towards me several thousand feet below, and I think, where on earth is this?

The Canadian city of 300,000 people that I live in is not one I ever heard about, growing up in Dublin. So sometimes when the small plane starts its descent, I find myself troubled by confusion, which gives way to a sense of arbitrariness. Why am I landing here, out of all possible spots on the turning globe? Why is this home? It's in my stomach that I register the protest, as the plane dips to the runway: what unfamiliar fields are these? I've gone astray, stepped off some invisible track that I was born to follow. How did I get here?

There is an answer: three beloved faces waiting for me in Arrivals. But the unease lingers.

By long tradition, Irish writers emigrate. Not always, of course, not nowadays—but still, many of us fly the coop. It's a small island, after all. It's rare to find Irish writers who haven't spent at least a few years abroad or who don't pass half their time at foreign universities. I've left for good twice, moving to England at twenty for a PhD, and to Canada at twenty-eight for love, and I've never regretted it. But still I wonder, what other lives might have awaited me at other airports? What chance or fate led me to this one?

The travelers in Virgil's *Aeneid,* quoted in the epigraph to this collection, complain of feeling "driven by the wind and the vast waves" and "ignorant of men and places." In my experience, migrants are awkward. Sometimes our self-consciousness can take the form of standoffishness. We want to be let in, yet keep our distance. We don't want to lose our accent, nor be mocked for it. We nurse a grudge, either suspecting the new country of not welcoming us, or expecting it to compensate us for all we've given up to get here.

As for settled folk, they have a long tradition of resenting newcomers. Those old towns that charm tourists today were shaped by the need to keep strangers where they belonged, outside the wall come nightfall, beyond the pale. Even worse were those who stayed on the move: such words as "vagabond," "vagrant," "drifter," made a crime of movement itself. The animal equivalent was "stray."

All we like sheep have gone astray, the sinners bleat in the Book of Isaiah (53:6). Straying has always had a moral meaning as well as a geographical one, and the two are connected. If your ethical compass is formed by the place you grow up, which way will its needle swing when you're far from home?

A stranger comes to town. That's one of the most reliable of plot motifs, and for a very practical reason: it's hard to describe a town if it's already banal to its inhabitants. The writer needs the stranger not just to set change in motion, but to reveal the town in all its peculiarity in the first place. Of course, put another way, what the town does is reveal all the strangeness in the stranger.

All this is my best explanation for why, on and off, for the past decade and a half, I've been writing stories about travels to, within, and occasionally from the United States and Canada. Most of these travelers are real people who left traces in the historical record; a few are characters I've invented to put a face on real incidents of border crossing. Many of them stray in several senses, when in the course of their journeys across geographical and political boundaries they find themselves stepping over other ones: law, sex, or race. Emigrants, immigrants, adventurers, and runaways— they fascinate me because they loiter on the margins, stripped of the markers of family and nation; they're out of place, out of their depth.

So many emigrations are at least semi-involuntary that I wanted to begin with a famous incident of resistance, a refusal to leave home. Crossing an ocean seems to me to be an act of daring, even if (in fact, perhaps especially if) you've got a gun to your head. Although Jumbo and his keeper Scott had to surrender all the comfortable routines of their life in London's Zoological Gardens, what they gained was what many travelers to North America have found over the centuries: room for reinvention. "Man and Boy" is about encountering foreignness, whether across the gulf of nationality or that of species. I see it as a love story—a rather queer one, about two different but mutually devoted mammals who find their only lasting sense of home in each other. (Scott's passionate phrasing about being "father and mother" to his "boy" Jumbo comes straight out of his ghostwritten *Autobiography*.)

To Caroline Thompson, the protagonist of "Onward," the motivation to emigrate is a wild hope of shedding nation and name in one go by starting all over again in Canada. I often write about prostitution because it is the *ur*-job, the job that symbolizes all other jobs. What drew me to Caroline's case was the peculiar discomfort of this trade carried on so domestically in a lower-middle-class household, visits from clients fitted in awkwardly between caring for her little girl and her brother. In the story I don't spell out the identity of the "distinguished gentleman" Fred wants to appeal to for help, because dropping such a famous name can be distracting. Charles Dickens, my favorite novelist, was a passionate liberal who believed in second chances. Where others would have seen a whore, he saw in Caroline a heroine who had endured much, about to sail into the unknown in pursuit of a new life.

Sometimes it is easier to write a story if you start by knowing very little about the characters: just a single spark to fall on the tinder. That was the case with "The Widow's Cruse," which is based on a single line from a newspaper. I love the idea that it is by parading her utter vulnerability in front of the male legal establishment that this woman manages to trick it into helping her commit an outrageous fraud. The gulf of misunderstanding between Huddlestone and Mrs. Gomez is as much about gender as religion; they share a nation but they will never be akin. He works to rise within the city's capitalist economy, whereas she, feeling perpetually foreign, resorts to crime and flight.

When I came across the murder that lies behind "Last Supper at Brown's," I thought it sounded like either Confederate-nightmare propaganda or wishful-thinking interracial romance...except that it happened. (Well, probably. No source is one hundred percent reliable.) I imagine Mrs. Brown, through the eyes of the desperate slave whom she persuades to take her along with him, as a wife who glimpses in the chaos of the Civil War a chance to end the private war of her marriage, and takes a step as bold as—and even more dangerous than—Mrs. Gomez in "The Widow's Cruse."

There is an Irish legend about the Hungry Grass, a patch of cursed land that, if you walk on it unawares, will fill you with perpetual hunger; that is a good image for how places hold on to the memory of pain. The notion probably dates from the Famine, the five years (1845–49), that left a massive scar across the Irish psyche. I have never known how to write about the Famine; it embarrasses me, partly because of the mawkish clichés it attracts and partly because I have no idea by what fluke or sleight of hand my own Catholic peasant ancestors came through it when so many of their neighbors rotted in the ditches. I only found a way into the subject when I happened across the letters of an Irishwoman who settled in London, Ontario, a century and a half before I did.

Jane and Henry Johnson in "Counting the Days" are Protestants, and not starving, but they leave Ireland in a bad time for much the same reason their poorer neighbors are crowding in their thousands onto the coffin ships. "Economic migrants," as we say nowadays, a cold phrase for a passionate wish for a better life—the same drive that would catapult most of my maternal grandfather's twenty siblings out of Ireland later in the nineteenth century. Out of a mixture of dread and hope, people will always migrate for the chance of a halfway decent life for themselves, and above all, their children—no matter how terrible the journey. Whenever I read headlines about human traffic gunned down crossing a border, or found suffocated in container trucks, I think of the Johnsons.

But what drew me into Jane and Henry's letters was not the description of the Atlantic crossing, but something rarer—the sense of a living, breathing marriage. The tensions are audible, but love beats like a pulse between the lines. Thousands of miles apart, husband and wife are welded together through their letters; the irony every history lover knows is that distance is what preserves, by pinning emotion onto paper. Focusing on Henry's last day, I wanted to bring the romantic and the hideous cheek by jowl, to try to capture the way in which such journeys as Jane's have something about them of both hell and heaven.

Temporary migrations within North America, such as the one in "Snowblind," could mean just as overwhelming a change of life as crossing the Atlantic. The Yukon, to most of the "tenderfeet" who tried their luck there, might as well have been another planet, not only due to its daunting climate but also because of its peculiar social codes; for all the lack of fences, it had something in common with a men's prison. When I learned the dark joke of gold rushes—that it is generally the shopkeepers who make their fortunes, not the miners—it occurred to me to wonder how a partnership between two very young men might have been strained to the breaking point by the opposing forces of ambition and realism.

Jensen, the nameless prospector I invented a handle for in "The Long Way Home," has come to find marriage less a partnership than a crippling burden. On a long bender, he tries to shrug off the weight of responsibility for hungry children. It's a pleasing irony—and one Mollie Monroe would have admitted—that it was this hellion, long since gone astray from domestic womanhood, who on this occasion went to such trouble to haul a prodigal husband home.

What fascinates me about Swegles, alias Morrissey, in "The Body Swap" is that he is clearly more akin to the counterfeiters he lives among (if undercover) than to the detectives for whom he works. For this freemasonry of peripatetic con men, the prison system seems to have been like a home to which they were always being forcibly returned, and freedom meant staying on the move, always incognito: a life in transit not just between places but between identities.

Children don't decide where to live, or what ventures are worth the risk; they get sent around the world as helplessly as parcels. While Lily May Bell, aka Mabel Bassett, zigzags her way west in "The Gift," both her birth mother and her adoptive father repeatedly stake their claim to her in correspondence with an intimidating bureaucracy. As a mother, I grit my teeth to think of Sarah losing her child forever because she was once poor. As a mother, again, I defend the Bassetts when they insist on the primacy of their de facto, hands-on parenting. So "The Gift" is an epistolary duet between rivals who never address each other directly, because I could think of no other way to honor their bitterly irreconcilable demands to be the girl's family.

Sometimes settling in seems almost impossible for emigrants, especially if their destination keeps failing to live up to the Promised Land of their imagination. The Puritans, for instance, soon discovered in the "virgin territory" of New England all the horrors they thought they'd left behind in Europe. Like "stray," the word "lost" has always had a moral meaning as well as a spatial one. The ultimate punishment, in Puritan communities, was to be banished, sent into a literal wilderness that matched what they saw as the spiritual wasteland of the sinner's heart. "The Lost Seed" is the opposite of a story I meant to write: its inverted mirror image. For years I was intrigued by an odd incident in which two women in Massachusetts were charged with being "lewd" together on a bed. But when I tracked down the source, what began to fascinate me was not the accused but their accuser. Fiction does that, in fact that is one of its most radical strengths; it disrupts the writer's sympathies as much as the readers'.

A particularly liberating thing about historical fiction is

that people rarely guess how autobiographical it can be. I wrote "The Lost Seed" as a shell-shocked immigrant during my first winter in Ontario, when, exactly as Berry remarks, the icicles hung over my front door like swords pointed at my head. "Vanitas," by contrast, came out of a trip I made through rural Louisiana. In my story, Aimée Loucoul's whole French Creole clan define themselves by reference to the home country for which they yearn; the cult of Frenchness is their true vanity. If travel is a stay-at-home girl's fantasy, nostalgia for a lost Eden can be a family's blight.

Whether in the form of military campaigns or the consequent flight of refugees, war is the root of many journeys. For "The Hunt," a story about the contemporary-seeming topics of child soldiers and rape as a war crime, I went all the way back to 1776. When you are uprooted from your familiar landscape, and from your home culture, how can you hold on to your sense of what's right? By telling the story of this fictional boy and girl during a terrible historical moment, I wanted to ask about what it means to be (paradoxically) an unpaid mercenary, sold into service in a far country; about the ethics of obeying orders; about victims who have themselves betrayed others.

Sometimes it is someone else's journey, someone else's decisions, that leave a thumbprint on your life. What haunts me about Minnie Hall in "Daddy's Girl" is the idea of a life lived in a strong character's turbulent wake; Minnie's path is shaped by her father's complicated prior journey. Like Mabel in "The Gift," Minnie has to live with a parent's commitment to a secret; she will never know where she came from, nor where Murray did, nor what lay behind Murray's decision to cross over the highly policed border of sex. So often these tales of emigration turn into tales of transformation, as if changing place is just a cover for changing yourself.

The sculptors in my last story, "What Remains," have lived and worked together all their lives until the moment Queenie goes ahead of Florence, straying across the line between clarity and confusion. As in "Counting the Days," this is a story about a couple divided, not by space this time but by a more painful alienation. Florence tries to bridge that terrible distance by means of love and memory, reckoning both the sum of what their long shared life amounts to and the dwindling total of "what remains."

Her task reminds me of my own. When you work in the hybrid form of historical fiction, there will be Seven-League-Boot moments: crucial facts joyfully uncovered in dusty archives and online databases, as well as great leaps of insight and imagination. But you will also be haunted by a looming absence: the shadowy mass of all that's been lost, that can never be recovered.

Unease. Wonder. Melancholy. Irritation. Relief. Shame. Absentmindedness. Nostalgia. Self-righteousness. Guilt. Travelers know all the confusion of the human condition in concentrated form. Migration is mortality by another name, the itch we can't scratch. Perhaps because moving far away to some arbitrary spot simply highlights the arbitrariness of getting born into this particular body in the first place: this contingent selfhood, this sole life.

Writing stories is my way of scratching that itch: my escape from the claustrophobia of individuality. It lets me, at least for a while, live more than one life, walk more than one path. Reading, of course, can do the same.

May the road rise with you.

Emma Donoghue
London, Ontario
2012

ACKNOWLEDGMENTS

"Man and Boy" was first published in *Granta* (the Fathers issue, ed. by Alex Clark, December 2008).

"The Widow's Cruse" first appeared in *One Story* (August 2012).

"Counting the Days" was first published in *Phoenix Irish Short Stories 1998,* ed. by David Marcus (London: Phoenix House, 1998), and broadcast on CBC Radio, May 2001.

"Snowblind" was first published in *The Faber Book of Best New Irish Stories,* ed. by David Marcus (London: Faber, 2007).

"The Body Swap" first appeared in *Princeton University Library Chronicle: Special Issue on Irish Prose* (2011).

Earlier versions of "The Lost Seed" were broadcast on BBC Radio 4 in May 2000 and published in *Groundswell: The Diva Book of Short Stories 2* (London: Diva Books, 2002).

"Vanitas" was first published in *Like a Charm: A Novel in Voices,* ed. by Karen Slaughter (London: Century and New York: William Morrow, 2004).

"The Hunt" first appeared in *The New Statesman,* January 2011, and was short-listed for the 2012 *Sunday Times* EFG Private Bank Short Story Award.

A slightly different version of "Daddy's Girl" was first published in *Neon Lit: The Time Out Book of New Writing,* ed. by Nicholas Royle (London: Quartet, 1998), and broadcast on BBC Radio 4, May 2000.

"What Remains" was first published in *Queens Quarterly* (spring 2001) and was shortlisted for the Journey Prize.

I would like to express my appreciation to all these editors, especially the late, great David Marcus. Also to Susan L. Johnson, whose essay "Sharing Bed and Board" sparked two of these stories, and to Scott Anderson at Sharlot Hall Museum and Christopher Dears, for going out of their way to help me with research inquiries for "The Long Way Home" and "Daddy's Girl" respectively.